DARK'S
TALE

DARK'S TALE

DEBORAH GRABIEN

EGMONT
USA

NEW YORK

EGMONT

We bring stories to life

First published by Egmont USA, 2010
443 Park Avenue South, Suite 806
New York, NY 10016

1 3 5 7 9 8 6 4 2

www.egmontusa.com
www.deborahgrabien.com

Library of Congress Cataloging-in-Publication Data

Grabien, Deborah.
Dark's tale / Deborah Grabien.
p. cm.
Summary: A cat abandoned in Golden Gate Park quickly learns how to take
care of itself, with the help of a street-smart raccoon and another stray cat.
ISBN 978-1-60684-037-5 (hardcover)
[1. Survival—Fiction. 2. Homelessness—Fiction.
3. Cats—Fiction. 4. Raccoon—Fiction. 5. Feral cats—Fiction.
6. San Francisco (Calif.)—Fiction.] I. Title.
PZ7.G7494Dar 2010
[Fic]—dc22
2009018117

Book design by Room39b

Printed in the United States of America

CPSIA tracking label information:
Random House Production
1745 Broadway • New York, NY 10019

For the people who work with the ferals.
And for Dark, Ivy, Carousel, Piglet,
and all our ferals, then and now.

ACKNOWLEDGMENTS

Thanks are due to the following WIP readers:
Sandra Larkin, Beverly Leoczko, Richard Furman,
Andrea Lindgren, Marty Grabien, Alex Lynch,
Moira Russell, Anne Weber, and a special thanks to
Natalie, for peppering me with questions that
helped make this suitable and hopefully interesting
to the age group I was writing for.

Also, the nice agent lady. Kate McKean gives
good feedback.

And Laura Anne Gilman,
for help with the afterword.

DARK'S
TALE

PROLOGUE

The first time I saw the Red Father, he was dancing in the moonlight and I thought he was a ghost.

He didn't see me, even though he probably knew I was there. Dogs—I wasn't sure what he was, but he looked like a dog to me—have good noses. Of course, right that moment, I wasn't sure he was really even there. That's how weird he looked.

It was long after moonrise and I was fifteen feet up a tree, settled in the crook where two branches came out together and then grew apart. I was covered by darkness and shadows and leaves, and I wasn't alone in the tree—there was a raccoon, higher up.

That tree-sharing thing happens a lot. I'd been in the park maybe a week, and I figured that out already.

It's a big park with a lot of trees, but some are better and safer than others. There's plenty to eat on the ground, but there are things on the ground that want to eat you. Sometimes, going up is the only thing that can keep you alive.

Tonight, the raccoon had passed me on the way up and we'd nodded at each other: *cool, no problem.* He wasn't a friend of mine, but unless there's food worth fighting over, the raccoons leave the rest of us alone, mostly.

Anyway, there he was down there—maybe a dog, maybe a ghost. I rested my chin on my paws and waited to see if he'd disappear, like smoke. It was possible. After all, the park's haunted. I was still a newbie then, and even I'd heard that.

But he didn't go anywhere. He lifted his face toward the sky, toward me and the raccoon and the moonlight, made this weird little noise—*snort-snort-snort, AHEEEOO!*—and began dancing.

It was amazing. He did this complicated, twisty, rhythmic thing with his neck; he looked like he was shaking water out of his ears. He slid his paws, moving like the kids who come into the park with their music and dance during the day. Difference was, he had four legs, and all the music was in his head.

He capered back and forth across the path. He kept it up for a few minutes, making weird little grunting noises, while I watched him and wondered what he was up to. The light from one of the park streetlights fell on his back. He had a black blob on the end of his tail, and then a white blob, and I suddenly realized what he was.

I'd heard there were foxes in the park, but this was the first one I'd seen. And he wasn't a ghost.

I shifted, watching him dancing all by himself down there, soaking up the moonlight. And then I tingled, prickled a little, because my ears had picked up noise, just as a smaller adult fox and four babies slipped out from under my tree. One minute he was alone and the next there were shadows, and there they were, lining up. His family had come out to dance with him.

They touched noses. It was very ceremonial, like a ritual of some kind. The family sat waiting, and Red Father went down the line, touching noses with each of them. It was funny but also moving. It made my heart ache. I wanted to be one of them, just for a moment.

Up above me, I heard a gentle little rumbling *mrmph*. The raccoon was snoring. I guess he wasn't a fan of dancing.

They'd just about finished touching noses when something caught their attention, and all their heads jerked toward the west: a car, coming up from Ocean Beach. I stayed where I was; up above, the raccoon rustled the leaves, then was quiet.

The Red Father moved. He barked, a sharp little noise, and then he was up and going, loping off into the undergrowth, leaving nothing behind to show anyone he'd been whirling and twirling in the moonlight just a moment ago. The others followed him, not making any noise at all. In the park, we understand about being quiet.

The car came and went, and I heard its noise die off in the distance. It was being driven too fast, the way most cars are when it's late and there's no one around to make them go slower. It had to be a Blank driving; the Blanks never look around them or see anything that doesn't jump out in front of them.

Of course, the night I saw the Red Father dancing, I was still learning the different names the animals in the park use for different groups of people. But I already knew about the Blanks, the people who come through the park without really looking around them. They were the first group I'd heard about.

I waited long enough to make sure there were none of the park's homeless people wandering around with their shopping carts full of junk, and no one with dogs off the leash. Then I slid down onto the grass, stretching, arching my back and flexing my claws.

Off to the south, a bird called out. It was an owl, and from the sound of it, something had come too close to its nest for comfort. I stayed where I was, tensed up, waiting to see if I had to move in a hurry. You don't want to annoy an owl. They'll rip the top of your head off.

The call lingered on the night air for a few seconds, and then it faded out. Late at night, when things are quiet, sound hangs on a little longer in the park.

Nice and quiet, nobody I could see. So I should have relaxed, but I couldn't—I suddenly had a strong feeling that I was being watched. It took me a minute, checking corners and dark patches with my eyes and ears, before I realized what it was: one of the park's homeless people, all the way across the road. Whoever it was, they were just standing there, not making any move toward me.

I let myself ease up. He or she was no threat to me, because there was no way I was visible, not from there.

The moon was all the way up now. In the buffalo paddock, there would be gophers, popping their heads out—it was their time of night. There was a gap in the fence, too small to let most things in or out, but I can make myself lean and long when I want to, and I could get through easily enough. I wouldn't do it during the day, not when the buffalo were out and grazing, but this was night, and night is my time.

No one was ever going to feed me again. Anything I ate, I had to learn how to catch; otherwise I was going to starve.

And maybe tonight, I'd figure out how to catch myself a gopher for dinner.

CHAPTER ONE

The night after I first saw the foxes, I actually did manage to figure out how to grab a gopher.

Hunting is all about instinct, and instinct can get rusty if you live indoors. But you keep it anyway, because you never know if the People you've lived with all your life will decide you're making their kid sneeze and dump you in the middle of a city park when no one is watching. Just because you don't have to find and kill your own food, that doesn't mean you should forget how to do it.

Besides, when I lived indoors, I used to catch and eat bugs. That made the People happy, because they were scared their child might get stung; once, when the child was very new, it got stung by a bee and nearly died. So I made it my business to catch anything that flew through the windows. Personally, I was surprised they didn't put screens in their windows to keep the bugs out, but then, the People never seemed to have much sense. I'd loved them anyway, though.

It scared me, at first, how slow I felt. The first couple of days after they dumped me, I did a lot of practicing, and even after the bug-catching indoors, I needed to work on it. I went hungry, no food for nearly two days, until I discovered the Dumpsters. I did a lot of Dumpster-diving. There's plenty to eat out here, if the raccoons and the Cores don't beat you to it.

I didn't want to starve, but the first time I saw a small mob of raccoons biting at each other over who got what out of the Dumpster I'd been heading for, I decided to try for gophers. The park's got about a million of them, and they turned out to be a lot easier to catch than I thought at first. What happened was, I was sitting on the grass, in the little not-quite-meadow near the big stone sign that says AIDS MEMORIAL, and I felt something move, underground.

I went very still, waiting. Something was down

there; I could feel it. It was almost as if the ground itself was letting me know: *Pssst—hey, Dark, there's food down here, maybe a mouse or something, dinner, check it out, this is your lucky day.*

I walked, keeping quiet, one step after another, following the little pattering movements that were making the ground vibrate under my paws. It tunneled in a twisty line and I went right along with it, very light on my feet, not letting whatever it was know I was there. I was Dark and I was my own name, a part of the darkness that moment, unseen by anything, just moving along, waiting to feed . . .

The pattering stopped. Just ahead of me, I heard a tiny *whoomph!*, and out of nowhere, a little spray of dirt flew right up into the air and settled, making a mound. Another *whoomph*, more dirt. The mound was getting bigger. Whatever was making it was right there under me, digging, a body length away.

I flattened myself out, became part of the earth I was moving on. One leg forward, another, then the rear. Half a length, close enough to reach out and—

Right in the middle of the mound, a head popped out.

I wasn't thinking. I wasn't even aware I was moving. But I must have been, because one second I was looking at the mound, and the next there was dirt from the destroyed mound scattered everywhere and a dead gopher, its neck broken, dangling from my mouth. I could taste it, earth and fur and a coppery tang that might be blood.

"WOW-*ow*. Nice catch."

The voice came from right behind me, a harsh little chattery voice, very friendly. I must have jumped a mile. I went straight up and then down, turning in midair with the gopher still dangling from my mouth. My tail had fluffed out huge, and all the fur on my back was standing up in a ridge. I can't have looked very dignified.

He was sitting there on the grass, watching me with his head tilted. There are lots of raccoons in the park—too many, if you ask me. Getting them annoyed with you is a bad idea, because they can climb as well as cats, and that means they can chase you. I was still very nervous of them, back then.

"I'm sorry." He was a little guy, young and sort of goofy looking. I was too preoccupied with hanging on to my dinner to consider why. "Did I scare you? I don't scare anyone usually."

"That's okay." Standing there with all four legs planted and my dinner cooling off between my teeth, I realized why he looked so weird: he was missing most of the fur on his front legs, and all the fur on his tail. His back end was as bald as a possum. "But this is my gopher. Don't get any ideas."

"What?" He reared up on his hind legs, stretching his neck and looking around like a prairie dog, and settled himself back down. "I can't really hear you—you sound all shmooshy. It's okay to put the gopher down. I don't eat those things, not if I can help it."

"Sorry." I opened my mouth, and let go. The raccoon was right—I was mumbling, trying to talk around a mouthful of dead dinner. It was starting to get heavy anyway, hurting my jaws.

"I like watching hunters hunt. Um, if they aren't hunting me, I mean." I was starting to like his voice— he broke up certain short words, so that *hunt* became *HUH-unt*, and *name* became *NAY-ame*. "What's your name, cat?"

"Dark." He seemed friendly enough, and anyway, he didn't seem interested in stealing my dinner. Mostly, raccoons just waddle straight at you if you're eating something they want, and if you have half a brain, you'll back away fast and find something else to eat. This was the first time one of them had wandered over just to hang out and chat. "What about you? Do raccoons have names?"

"Well, sure. Everyone has names. Hello, Dark. I'm Rattail."

"Oh. Hi." Actually, it was a pretty good name. I could see why he was called that—that stripped-bald tail of his did remind me a little bit of a rat. It wouldn't have been polite or kind to say so, though. "Pleasure to meet you. Hey, you don't mind if I eat, do you? I was going to take it into the bushes. I don't want to attract attention."

"Please do." He watched me pick up the gopher and skittered along next to me. I'm not that big, and the raccoons I'd seen since the Dumping had mostly been lots bigger than me. Rattail wasn't, though. He was just about my size, only heavier. "So, were you born in the park? Because I was."

"No."

He must have seen me tense up. "Oh, I'm sorry—did I say something wrong? I didn't mean to."

"It's okay."

He was quiet, and I tore off a piece of gopher.

It wasn't okay, not really. I'd loved my life, loved having a big padded cushion to sleep on and an eating bowl with a picture of a cat on it that looked like me. I missed the way the man would tickle my ears, and the way the woman used to laugh when I'd chase the feathers she'd dangled for me. I missed sleeping in a patch of sunlight without worrying if something was going to come after me, missed running down the hall when they came home, then rubbing up against their legs. When we rub, it's to mark our territory. I'd always thought the People were my territory, but I guess I'd been wrong.

So I must have stiffened up or something. My new friend had good eyes.

"Does it hurt? Would you rather not look at whatever it is?"

"No, I wasn't born here. I lived in a house, with a family. They dumped me here, about a week ago. Said I made their baby sneeze or something."

I sounded nice and steady, pushing the feeling away,

what I'd lost, not knowing why they would do that to me. I could have told him the truth. I could have said yes, it hurts and I'm not going to think about it right now and maybe not ever because why should I hurt myself and make myself crazy when I can't ever have it back?

But that would be admitting to things. Admitting it made it too real. And I couldn't afford to have it be too real, not while I was still trying to figure out how many gophers there were out here.

"Allergic?" Rattail sounded sad, like he'd heard it before. "That sucks. It happens a lot. Hey, have you met Casablanca? Pale creamy tabby cat, over near the Eighth Avenue entrance? No? Oh, you should. She still actually lives outside the park, goes back there when the weather's bad, I mean. Her people moved away and left her, but she knows how to get into the basement, and she sleeps there sometimes. Maybe I can hook you up."

I was done with the gopher, and just about to say yeah, sure, okay, when Rattail suddenly did that prairie-dog thing again, upright, back on his haunches.

"Dangers coming." He was moving, kind of a fast waddle. "Dangers with a dog, on the path. There's at least one Danger, maybe two of them. And the dog. Tree. Let's move."

"Dangers? Rattail, what are you—?"

"People." He booked it, heading for the nearest tree. "Bad. Nasty ones, crazy-bads. Dangers. Move it!"

I made it up the tree before he did. Something about the way he'd reacted to whatever was coming down the road toward us had caught my attention. My heart was slamming, going way too fast. Rattail worked his way onto the branch alongside me, and we hunkered down, side by side, watching and waiting. Dangers? Crazy-bads?

They came around the corner, two boys and a dog. And I knew, with one look, that Rattail had nailed it. "Danger" was the perfect word for them. They were wrong things. You could smell the wrongness. You could almost see it.

"Nightmare!" One of them was yelling at the dog, a big black thing. "Get back over here, you stupid dog!"

They'd stopped on the path. One of them was waiting, his hands in his pockets, and the other one was calling the dog. I looked down at them, watching them closely—I can see better in the dark than I do in the daytime. I could see into the big one, the one who was yelling at his dog. I could smell the bad and the crazy and the meanness coming off him in waves.

"Dangers." Rattail was very still next to me, grabbing the branch with all four paws, anchoring himself. "Shhh."

It was at least ten feet between the crazy-bads and the first branch. They couldn't get at us, and the dog, who'd come back to sit next to its crazy-bad Danger human, couldn't climb anyway. But Rattail was spooked, and I held still.

"You done scaring that dog, or what?" The first one was rocking back and forth on the balls of his feet. His voice wasn't mean, not like his friend's was. He just sounded bored. "Because I want to go hit the deli over on Haight."

About ten feet down the path, the strangest thing happened: the one who wanted a sandwich glanced over his shoulder, and up. He gave a tiny nod. I would have sworn there was a little smile on his face.

I couldn't see how it was possible, but I thought he knew we were there, Rattail and me.

They moved on. It wasn't until they were almost out of sight, had become distant shadows under the trees to the north, that I felt Rattail relax and my own muscles loosen up.

I turned on the branch. "They're called Dangers? Thanks for the warning. That's a good name for them, at least for the big one and his dog. Is everyone in the park like that?"

He twitched. "Not at all. All kinds of people live in the park. Most of them don't even know we're here. There's a group of nice ones who drive through pretty much every night and feed us. We call them Warms. Mostly we just get Blanks, the ones that think they're the only things alive in the park. But . . ."

He stopped, and was quiet. I prompted him. "But . . . ?"

"Dangers are everywhere." His shoulders twitched again. "It's not just people. Animals can be Dangers, too. I got sick for a while after another raccoon went for me—I was hot all the time, thirsty. He was crazy-mad and crazy-bad. Sharp teeth, too. I was lucky I healed up, because he was trying to kill me. I'm still waiting for the fur to grow back, where it fell out. Maybe it won't, though. It's growing very slow, and I'm not as fast as I used to be."

"And he was a Danger? That crazy-bad raccoon, I mean?" I put my front paws on the trunk of the tree and found the balance point. The two Dangers and their dog were long gone.

"He was my father." Rattail curled his bald tail under him for a moment, like he was trying to hide it. "There are ghosts in the park, too. Do you know about ghosts?"

"Yes—well, sort of. When they first dumped me, that first night, there was a skunk, out near the windmill. I was worried that he was going to spray me—we used to get skunks in our yard, and I remember what they smell like. But he said no, he didn't have any reason to spray me, and anyway there were worse things in the park to worry about. And he told me a little about ghosts. So I know there are ghosts in the park."

Ratty was balanced up behind me. "Ghosts—and other things. You can't always see them—there's things in the park that will trick you. But I think it's safe to head back down now. It's near feeding time. Want me to show you where the Warms put the dry food down every night?"

So I caught my first gopher, made my first friend, and learned how to smell danger. Not a bad night. And not too many nights later, I got to meet Casablanca and Memorie.

CHAPTER TWO

During the day, the park is a very different place.
I used to hear the People use that phrase—"as different as night and day"—but I never understood it
before. Two weeks in the park, and I was coming to
understand just what it meant, and how true it is.

We were halfway up the tree I'd chosen to live in
mostly, across JFK Drive from the back of the new
museum. It was a warm sunny day, and it felt like
just about everyone in the world was down there,
Dangers and Blanks and maybe some Warms, too.

"Rattail? Can I ask you something?" No one seemed
to know we were up there, a cat and a raccoon. It was
secret. We were secret. And I like secrets.

"Sure. Is it personal?"

"No, it's about ghosts, sort of. Remember that first night I met you, when I caught the gopher, and we were talking about ghosts, and about how the park was haunted? You said there were other things, things that would trick me. What did you mean?"

Down below us, two children were being taught how to ride their bicycles. They didn't seem to be doing very well, because they kept falling off.

"I meant what I said, that's what. There are ghosts in the park, and there are things that will confuse you, make you think they're something they really aren't. Trickster things."

I turned around and began washing him. It was weird, me wanting to do that. I never had any kittens, and after I went to the vet one time with the People, I never wanted to have kittens, but for some reason, washing Rattail as if he were a kitten felt nice, and normal, and right.

"What kind of ghosts?" I asked him around a mouthful of dark fur. "Ghosts of raccoons or cats, you mean? Or of other things? And what kind of trickster things?"

"It's hard to say. Hard to tell what those spirits came

from, and I don't know too much about the tricksters, just that they're here. You could ask Memorie." He sounded very wary suddenly, as if he was afraid I was making fun of him.

"Who—?"

I stopped. Down below, one of the two kids, the smaller one, had fallen off her bicycle with a solid thump, landing on the path hard enough to make her cry. I could hear her wailing, thin and high and unpleasant, and for a bad moment, I could hear the child the People had produced, the one who always sneezed and came up red and rashy when I was anywhere near it. I didn't want to think about that child. I'd liked it well enough, but it cost me my home. That thought brought me back to where I'd been, what I wanted to know.

"Who's Memorie?" It was a weird name, I thought.

"She's my friend." That odd little lilt he had in his voice was very strong. "She's very old. She's been in the park a long time—years and years."

"Oh." I put a paw on Ratty and went right on washing. "Is she a raccoon?"

"She's an owl, very old. She knows most things that happen here in the park."

"Really? You have an owl for a friend?"

He shifted, showing me his other side, and I began to wash there. His fur was bristly at the ends, soft at the base, almost oily. That fur must be why raccoons don't seem to feel the weather so much. His voice dropped suddenly, the chatter becoming thin and faraway. "Yes, I do. And she knows where all the ghosts are, and maybe all the tricksters, too."

I didn't say anything for a minute. It wasn't that I didn't believe in ghosts—I don't know whether I did or not. But it was going to take me a minute to process what Rattail was saying. Raccoons and cats, that's weird enough. But a raccoon and an owl? Was he joking?

I'd forgotten to lick, and he leaned into me and nudged, a nice clear signal: *Don't stop doing that.* "I'll introduce you to her, if she wants me to. I have to ask her first. She'll probably say it's okay, but I have to ask."

"Sounds good to me."

I went back to washing. I was purring, too. Rattail

loved hearing me purr; it's something raccoons can't do. Once he'd figured out that the growly noise was a happy one, he'd decided he'd liked it.

"When do you want me to ask her?"

"Maybe tonight? I told Casablanca I'd meet her at the bench where the Warms feed us. Hey, is it true the Warms leave food every night, even if it rains?"

"Yes, they do." Rattail was relaxed again, sprawled out on his belly with all four legs dangling over the sides of the branch. "They put out dry for me, too. I can't stand that wet stuff. The foxes like it, though. So you might have to share it with the Red Father or some of his family, if they come by."

I shivered, just a little. I didn't like the idea of having to go nose to nose with the foxes to see who got dinner. I had a feeling I could spend a lot of time going hungry, if that happened. "Any way to avoid that? Come on, Rattail, share. I'm new at this."

"Well, I just back off when they show up—that works. Red Father's pretty calm for a fox, so long as you don't threaten his family. 'Blanca eats as much as she can while the Warms are still there, because the foxes wait until the people leave. But some nights, the

Warms don't wait, they just put out the food and go. So it's smart to always eat fast, especially if you want the wet food more than the dry."

He gave me a mournful look—I'd stopped washing him. "Where are you going?"

"Bathroom. I'll be right back."

I'd already marked out spots along my usual routes, spots I could reach from my tree. It's like everything else about living out here. You do what you need to do, you do it fast, and you always keep your senses working. That's the way to stay alive.

And since I'd figured out the best way to stay alive, wouldn't you think I'd have had enough sense to follow my own rules? But I didn't.

I was burying my business behind a dead stump and listening to the traffic on Fulton Street going by just a few feet away. There was something about the traffic that has a rhythm to it, and if you listen to it too closely, you stop hearing any other sounds. It's as if you're getting into some kind of trance where your senses don't work right. I guess that was why I didn't hear the dog until it was too close.

I got lucky; it was a big heavy thing. It was the

movement of the ground beneath my feet that made me wake up, jump for the clear path and the dense bushes on the other side.

I hit the first tree I came to and jumped for the lower boughs. The dog was right behind me. I could feel it panting, imagine it drooling and slavering, excited because it thought it was going to catch me, kill me . . .

"Chalky! Bad dog! Down!"

There was his owner, a girl on Rollerblades, with plastic cups protecting her knees. I stared down at them, shaking, and watched her clip a leash on the dog's collar. She pulled at him, but she had to pull hard to make him move. He was staring up at me, and he didn't want to leave.

Casablanca had told me something that made me think: every Blank could turn out to be a Danger or a Warm. The problem is, you can't tell from looking at them. That's too bad, because walking up to someone and rubbing their ankles might lead to a new home and a way out of the park. But what if they turned out to be a Danger instead? It wasn't worth the risk.

This time, I checked every direction before I came

down and headed back to Ratty. We stayed there, snoozing away the afternoon, until the sky began changing color and the crowds of people on the paths thinned out.

A few minutes after Ratty left to find out if his owl friend wanted to meet me, Casablanca showed up. I didn't see her at first. She's that dusty color the grass turns when it hasn't rained for a while. Besides, I got distracted by a trail of gopher mounds. They looked fresh, but tonight I was supposed to be formally introduced to the Warms who fed Casablanca. That would mean food I didn't have to hunt for, and I wanted to be nice and hungry for that. I'd been eating the leftovers for a couple of days, but the Warms hadn't seen me yet, and Casablanca and Rattail both told me that looking hungry and underfed and pathetic makes the Warms want to feed you more.

"Hi, you." She'd been curled up in the bushes, watching the world go by, perfectly blended in.

I could feel the gophers moving underground, and my whiskers were twitching. *No chasing the gophers*, I told myself. *You want to stay hungry until the Warms get here.* "Hi back. Anything going on?"

"Some things." Casablanca always seemed to be listening, paying attention, instead of talking. "Heard some Core talking about a new animal in the park. Sounded scary-bad. We have to watch."

The Cores, the people who live in the park—they're mostly young, and they had no homes they could go to. I avoid them, because I avoid anything I'm not familiar with, but also because most of them have dogs. Besides, the Cores can get kind of nuts. They do stuff the Blanks don't seem to do—not outdoors, anyway.

But crazy or not, they have a way of knowing just what's happening in the park, and they pick up the news before anyone else does. So if Casablanca had heard the Cores talking, it was something that was going to affect us all.

"What about scary-bad animals?"

"The Cores were talking." She was sitting with her paws out in front of her, not tucked. Maybe she wasn't all that relaxed after all. "Two of them. Right here last night—I was waiting for the Warms, and these two Cores came by and sat down."

She jerked her head, up and behind. "I went up— that's my tree. I heard them. I'd seen them before;

they always had a dog with them—a puppy, really. No puppy last night, and they were talking about it. The scary-bad animal got the puppy."

"Some new animal got the puppy? You mean, hurt it?"

"Ate it." Her fur rippled suddenly, a tremor like the wind over the grass. "It ate the puppy. One of the Cores was crying. The other was saying bad things, things he wanted to do about it, about how the Blanks don't care and won't do anything to help or stop it. He talked about knives and guns and what he wanted to do. They said . . ."

She stopped. I waited.

"He named it. The scary-bad animal, I mean." She was being very quiet, the barest whisper under the trees and the night sky. "He called it a coyote. I never heard of that. You?"

So that was why she'd told me so much; I got it now. She was hoping I had some information to share; it was supposed to be a trade, but I had nothing to give her. "No. Never. Coyote? I wonder if that's what they're all called, or if that was the name of the one that ate the puppy?"

"All of them, I think. The angry Core boy—the one who said the Blanks wouldn't help and that he wanted to do bad stuff to them—he said 'those miserable coyotes.'"

I stared at her. She looked at me, and I saw her eyes, shining golden in the dark.

"We have to be careful, Dark. But I don't know what to be careful of, because I don't know what they look like. Not yet."

She was right. It was going to make things tricky, not knowing what we were supposed to be afraid of, or watching out for. All the things in the park that I thought of as scary were some kind of dog, like the foxes, or the pitbulls and terriers most of the Cores had. But this thing, this coyote, it ate dogs. This was a whole new variety of scary-bad. . . .

"Up!" Casablanca was streaking for the shadows behind the bench; somewhere down the path, I heard people's voices, and footsteps coming close.

I slid in and hunkered down next to 'Blanca, completely covered by the bushes, as they turned down the path and sat on the bench not more than five feet away. I could smell something wafting back at me on the night breeze. I was sniffing hard, trying to identify it. It was familiar. I'd smelled this before. Something the People had used . . .

Casablanca stared out at them. They were passing something back and forth. "Same two Cores. They've been drinking—see that bottle? I don't know what it is, but it makes them loud." Her neck was stretched, hard and taut. "Listen."

". . . you hear about Jackie? Yeah, you know her— that skinny chick from Idaho, set up out near the tulip garden near the beach. The one with the tats? Yeah, she says she saw coyotes out there. Man, there were two of them, right there, like, five feet away from her. She said the gardeners found parts of something the coyotes killed—might be a cat, or a skunk . . ."

I wasn't moving—not a whisker, not my tail, nothing at all. Something out there, something new, something Danger. And I couldn't understand it.

We stayed off each other's turf. The cats didn't hassle the raccoons, the raccoons didn't hassle the foxes, the foxes left the skunks alone, the skunks didn't mess with the possums. The predatory birds, things like hawks and owls, stuck with mice and rats and gophers and voles. Down on the ground, even fights over the available food were pretty rare, except among ourselves—the raccoons argued with the other raccoons. It was a system, and even as new to the park as I was, I could see why it worked. We respected each other. That was how we all stayed alive.

But here was a new thing, new to the park, a new kind of Danger. What kind of animal was so stupid that it didn't see the only way the park would keep working for all of us was if no one messed up the balance . . . ?

"Showtime. This should be interesting." Casablanca had picked up the sound of a car engine.

I'd heard the car coming up, just as Casablanca had; she must have recognized it. It was a black car, pulling up next to the curb. I could see two people in it. The engine died, the door opened, and I saw a man get out, tallish, solid. "Is this the Warms? Will they feed us even with the Cores sitting there?"

"Watch." She was back to one-wording me. "Watch."

"Hi, look, sorry, but can we ask you to move? We feed the park animals right where you're sitting. Thanks, man. Do you guys need some spare change? Thanks . . . Casablanca! Here, kitty . . ."

The Cores were moving, heading west and away. Casablanca slipped through the brush and out to the bench, talking, letting them know she was there. I was right behind her.

"Hi, Casablanca, pretty girl, dinnertime . . . Whoa! Where'd you come from? Jack, look, there's a new cat, coal black. . . ."

I hung back a little, being cautious. I was letting them look at me, but I was absorbing them, too—the way they spoke, moved, smelled.

Casablanca was on the path, rolling and scent-marking; it was pretty obvious these were people even Casablanca trusted. The woman was watching her, smiling. It was a real smile, the kind I'd seen before. I wondered why they didn't just take Casablanca home with them, since they obviously loved cats.

"Angie, check out the new one, she looks totally black. Really dark. Here, dark, dark, Dark . . ."

I stepped forward, just an inch or two. There was fog coming in, moving through the treetops, beginning to settle on the road and the grass. The woman, Angie, was pouring dry cat food into small piles, more than enough for both Casablanca and me. That seemed funny, but the man said something about the "little bandits," and then I remembered what Rattail had said, about the Warms leaving food for the raccoons.

Angie opened two cans of wet food and dumped them out. I could feel myself wanting to drool. Fish— there was fish in it, my favorite. I let myself move a bit closer, and out of nowhere, I found myself wanting to curl around Angie's ankles.

"Damn, it's getting cold out here. Here, kitty, come get your dinner."

We settled down to eat. I remembered what Rattail had told me earlier, about eating as fast as possible. The Warms had been gone only a few minutes, and Casablanca and I had each almost demolished our piles, when Rattail came skittering up.

"Hey." He sat down at a pile of straight dry next to me and began picking up individual pieces of kibble and popping them into his mouth. Raccoons don't have paws, they have hands, with thumbs on them, almost like people. "Hi, Casablanca. Dark, I saw Memorie and she says yes, I should bring you to meet her." He took a mouthful, chewed, and swallowed. "No hurry. Whenever we're done."

CHAPTER THREE

If you asked me before the Dumping to give you a list of things I was ever planning to do, climbing a tree to talk to an owl wouldn't have made that list.

We finished eating and said good night to Casablanca. She nodded at me, told me to come by later, when it was closer to tomorrow morning. I asked her why, and she shared another secret: it seemed that her Warms weren't the only Warms in the park. There was another one, a woman, who came by just before sunrise every day to leave more food. I told her I didn't think I'd be hungry by then, but she just laughed at me.

She was right to laugh, and I knew it, after I thought about it for a minute or two. Food is never something you don't need. And food that you don't have to hunt for that comes to you because someone's willing to give it to you? You take it whenever it's offered.

"Casablanca's nice." Rattail was scuttling along, me right behind. We were keeping to the edge of the paths, the bushes never too far away to duck into, in case we needed some cover fast.

"I like her, too. Look, Ratty, I need to ask you about Memorie. I've never had anything to do with an owl before—birds and cats, well, we don't usually social-ize. Usually they're food. Is there anything I should know? Anything I ought to do or not do, maybe?"

"Yes, sort of." He stopped, looking both ways for oncoming car headlights. The darkness was steady and undisturbed, all clear except for the pale glow of the streetlamps. We crossed the street. Wherever Memorie lived, it was off my usual turf. "You have to be calm. You can't show her tense muscles. And no staring. We're going to be guests, and owls don't like it if you stare at them. Memorie doesn't, anyway."

He headed into the trees, me right at his heels. I was quiet, thinking about it. It made sense. Owls are pretty fierce, and they're hunters. They hunt a lot of the same food cats do, so on that level, we were competitors, me and Memorie.

That was where things got confusing for me. If Memorie had been a cat, handling the situation would be straightforward, with both of us knowing the rules. There would be a big staring contest, measuring each other up, figuring out which of us was the alpha female.

But that wasn't happening tonight. Memorie wasn't a cat. I was meeting her on her own turf, and she was going to have the advantage. This wasn't neutral ground. So I had to let her know I understood she was the alpha there. I just hoped I could be convincing about it.

I took a moment to thank Bastet for the fact that cats are born with good manners. I'm not really too sure who or what Bastet is, except that apparently, she was a very important cat, sometime and somewhere. But thanking her for things that are useful to me, that's ritual. I was born knowing I was supposed to thank her. Don't ask me how.

"Here we are."

"Memorie lives up there?" I was up on my hind

legs with my front paws balanced against the rough bark, craning my neck. "Smart. If I wanted to build a nest, I'd pick a tree like this one. Easier to defend. She must have a lot of sense."

"I'll go first." He wasn't really replying to what I'd said—he was nervous, edgy. "She knows me. It's safer this way. You follow on behind, okay? Dark? What is it? Why did your tail just puff up? What's going on?"

"I don't know. Something—I think something's watching me." Eyes, I thought. No way to tell whose eyes, or where they were. There was nothing anywhere near me threatening enough to have caused everything to tense up: the back end of the new aquarium, some old tarps, a bundle of rags across the street, a pair of old shoes someone had thrown out in the road, shadows moving and rustling in the grove behind us . . .

"Are you going to just wait and see if something comes out? Because we shouldn't make Memorie wait. She won't like that."

"No." Nothing, just the bundle of rags moving a little in the wind. "You go first—I'll follow."

Up the tree, up into the hidden perches and the full darkness, little stray moments of light falling where the leaves happened to thin out. The fog was going to come in soon, and a mist was already rising from the wet grass down below, where the park's sprinkler systems had come on. I could feel the damp in my joints.

I heard Memorie before I saw her, or maybe it was just instinct again, lifting all the hairs along the ridge of my spine. I paused for a moment, getting control over myself. Okay, so I was on her turf. She'd invited me, and that meant I could just lay that spooked fur right back down where it belonged. There was no reason to feel so vulnerable.

And it was okay, my hesitation, because it gave Rattail a chance to get up there before me. Maybe she thought I was hanging back because I was scared of her, or maybe awed by her. Probably not, though. If she was half as old or half as smart as Rattail said she was, she had time to have learned that cats don't get awed by much.

Still, now that we were near the top, I didn't mind hanging around, waiting for Rattail to tell me that everything was good and it was okay for me to come up. Besides, it gave me the chance to look around and see if I could figure out why I'd felt eyes on me.

I peered down from my high perch. The ground looked miles away from up there, but I caught movement: something small and pale was scurrying across the grass, making a dash for cover. A vole, a young possum, maybe a rat. It was too big to be a mouse. Cats aren't the only ones who get dumped here. It happens to pet rats, hamsters, rabbits, sometimes even lizards or snakes.

One thing was for sure, though: whatever that was scooting for cover down there, it wasn't long for the world. If you're something an owl eats, you don't nest at the foot of an owl's tree. That's just stupid.

"Dark?" Rattail was upside down, his head dangling from a dense cluster of leaves. "Memorie says please come up now."

I turned to climb. I guess part of me was still thinking about that feeling of being watched, because even though I was concentrating on Memorie, I noticed a difference on the ground below. The pile of rags was gone.

Memorie was sitting in a bowl.

It wasn't quite like the kind of bowl the People used to put my food in; it was shaped sort of like that, but it was much larger. I took a second look and suddenly realized she was sitting in a nest. It was a bowl made of sticks, leaves, and dead grass.

I must have stared at it a little too long, because Memorie spoke up. "You are looking at my nest."

Her voice was a lot higher than I would have expected. Something about her made me think her voice would be deep, but instead, there was a pale thin note. She sounded like part of the wind. "I did not build it," she told me. "Once, it belonged to some-one else. Now it is mine."

"It's very nice." I was still trying to fit the voice to the body it was coming from, and I couldn't quite do it. "Who was the someone else? Another owl?"

"No." The more she spoke, the stranger she sounded to me. You could hear every muscle she used to vocal-ize, nice and clear, but you couldn't have heard her more than a branch away. "My kind do not eat each other, or drive each other off. There are owls who will do such things, but not those of my breed. This was a nest of crows. No longer." Her voice whistled away, a high reedy breath carried off into the night sky. "Mine."

Don't stare, I told myself, but that was trickier than it sounds. "I understand. Thank you for inviting me to meet you, Memorie. This is a great honor."

I'm not formal, not usually. But sitting in that tree, the words just came, and they were the right ones. I could tell, and so could she. There had been that moment of caution—her words and how I reacted to them—and the reaction had been correct. I could meet her eye now, study her, see who and what she was, with no fear of misunderstanding.

I'd seen owls hunting before, since the Dumping. They're amazing when they want food. You get no warning, just a sudden cold chill at the base of your nerves. Then a rush of wind, real wind, wings just a few feet over your head, the owl sweeping down the length of a field, great wings out to catch and manipulate the air. There's a squeak and then silence, and then that fast, scary rush of wings again, disappearing back into the canopy and the darkness.

So I studied her, not staring in a way that might make her think I was challenging her, just checking her out. My first thought was that owls, if they all looked like Memorie, were about the weirdest-looking things ever.

For one thing, she was as tall as I am. I was sitting upright on the branch—I wasn't about to challenge her, but I wasn't going to lay down and worship at her feet, either. I was opposite her, and we were eye to eye. That was one big bird.

My second thought was that she was as beautiful as she was spooky. Most birds look round to me, but Memorie was long and lean and elegant. There was something about the way her shoulders moved, about the talons holding on to the edge of the stick nest as if it were the sturdiest perch in the whole park, that made me think that if owls got nine lives, she might come back as a cat in one of them.

The spookiest thing was that she had a face inside a face, separated by a ridge of feathers shaped like a heart. That was dark, but the face inside, the feathers behind her golden eyes and black scary-sharp beak, was the color of the syrup the People use to put on their pancakes in the morning. Right down the middle, dividing the amber pool of color in half, was a strip of soft, pale feathers, very buff-colored and fine.

Plus, she had ears. Birds don't usually have ears, not like this—they were huge things, sticking straight up. She could probably have heard a vole twitching its whiskers half a mile away if—

"Wait for me."

I was so surprised, I nearly fell out of the tree. Her head had turned almost all the way around on her shoulders. I scrabbled, got my claws back into the branch, and watched as she suddenly seemed to fall off the edge of that stolen nest. For a horrible moment, I thought she was going to crash, just hit the ground far below.

But of course, she didn't. Ten feet down, the wings were there, wide and beautiful, and she was moving, riding the wind, straight and flat and sure. I watched, with Rattail next to me. Inside I was cheering her on. There's something beautiful about a perfect kill, so long as you aren't the one getting killed.

She tilted. It was amazing: she was in flight, her whole body going one way, and she changed direction midair. I saw her legs extend, caught a glint of dwindling moonlight as it touched the killing talons, as they found and caught and gripped.

And I heard her. This was no thin little whisper—this was a scream of triumph, a victory call, letting every hunter under cover of the night know that she had taken to the air and taken what she needed. There was no one and nothing within a few miles in every direction who didn't hear the scream and understand what it meant.

A rush of wings, a ghostly rustle. She was back, landing a little awkwardly because she could only use one foot. The other set of talons had a young possum clutched hard and dangling. It was dead and bloody, and ready to be dinner.

"Wow." It just came out, nice and spontaneous, a tribute from one hunter to another. "*Wow.*"

After that, of course, we were friends, or at least we understood each other. Rattail relaxed, the owl ate her supper, and I waited. There were questions I wanted answers to, but you don't interrupt a hunter while she's eating. I let her finish the possum, tail and all, before I spoke up. I knew what I wanted to say, and I was picking my words very carefully.

"Rattail told me you've lived in the park for a long time. He says you're very wise, and that you know more than anyone about what happens in the park. If that's true, is it all right if I ask you a question or two? Because I haven't been here long, and if I'm going to stay here, there are certain things I need to know."

"Ask." The amber heart, with its pale hourglass and huge yellow stare, turned my way. "My eyes see far, and my ears hear deep. Look down now, and you will see what I have seen already—the shadow of the Red Father, passing below us with his clan. My kind sees much, and more, and most. So if an answer is mine, it will be yours, as well. Ask."

We were eye to eye now, green to gold, not locked in challenge, just acknowledging each other. I hadn't glanced down toward the ground, hadn't taken that challenge, because there was no need. It wasn't that I didn't believe her, but I didn't feel any need to tell her that I'd already noticed the fox tribe passing beneath the tree, registered it and filed it away in my mind, just before she mentioned them. "Rattail told me the Park is haunted. He said you know where the ghosts are, and who. And he said there are other things here."

"Ghosts. Yes. There are ghosts here. Some animal, some human." She stopped and did that bizarre head-swivel thing again. "One in particular, both, perhaps neither—I am never sure which."

Something went down my spine. Memorie's voice hadn't changed, but out of nowhere, I heard a warning. Next to me, Rattail was quiet, not moving.

"I don't understand you. What do you mean, please, Memorie? Both human and animal?"

Her ears lifted suddenly, straight up, and settled again. "He is the Bringer and the Taker. Hope that you wait all nine of your lives before you see him, cat. For when he comes, you go with him, or go alone. When he is there for you, when you hear his music and he lets you see him with all masks forsaken, you will know that all your choices are made and over with."

My shoulders were rippling, and there was noise wanting out of me, a long low growl of warning. "Bringer. Taker. His music, you say? What music is this?"

"The voice of wind on water. Of earth and fire, coming through tree."

Was that a singsong I was hearing? It reminded me of when the People had first brought home their child, how the woman would sit with it in her lap, singing to it, willing it to sleep. Yes, a singsong, and Memorie went on.

"Everywhere and nowhere, and no place to hide. He means you no harm, but he is Bringer and Taker and you should hope to never sense him near or hear him, until your choices all are made. What else did you wish to ask of me, cat?"

"Well." I forced the hair on my tail to stay smooth. It wasn't that I didn't trust her, but I'm a hunter and a predator and I don't willingly show another hunter my own unease. "If you don't mind, Memorie, I'd like to ask you: what do you know about a hunter, maybe a kind of dog, called a coyote?"

"Coyote. You speak of the trickster?"

I blinked at her. "Trickster? I don't know, Memorie. The name I heard was coyote. What do you mean?"

She opened her beak and lifted her wings, arching and spreading. Suddenly, just for a moment, she was huge, entirely different in shape and size and presence. Everything about her felt as if she'd been wearing some kind of mask over her whole body, and now she'd peeled it back. Or maybe it was the other way around, and this new big different scary-bad owl was the mask.

"What do I mean?" She settled down, and she was Memorie again, a different bird, a different shape in the dark. "What do you see, cat? Do you believe your eyes? Can you trust them to tell you the truth?"

"I don't understand." It was a lie—I did understand. But the understanding was down along my nerves, not in my head, and I needed to know more.

"Yes, I know of coyotes. They walk as I fly, far and long. There are mountains to the south of here, and mountains to the north. They came from there, walking, stopping to take what they chose along the way. Once, a long time in the past, they were here. If they have come again, it will mean no good for anyone here. You will know them when you see them, and when you see them, trust your muscles and be prepared to fly."

CHAPTER FOUR

After that conversation with Memorie, Rattail went off to do whatever raccoons like to do when there's no cats around, and I went looking for a safe, quiet place to curl up. Memorie had left me with a lot to think about.

I found a quiet patch of dirt, about halfway between Memorie's tree and 'Blanca's feeding spot. The bushes grew densely here, the branches tangled together. That made it pretty safe for me, since a dog or a fox or a coyote would still be trying to figure out how to get at me from one side while I was hustling out the back. I still had no real picture of a coyote in my head—all Memorie had told us was that they looked sort of like dogs, from the same family—but

I figured that if it was big enough to eat someone's puppy, it was probably too big to get in where I hunkered down without ripping its nose to shreds.

I curled up, and thought. My eyes were wide open—I don't have to close them to think—and I was thinking hard. What was it Memorie had said?

They came from a different place, these dogs who are more than dogs.

Okay, so they weren't from here. But Memorie had made it sound as if the coyotes had come from very far away. I could hear her voice in my head, thin and high and trailing away into the breeze like pollen: *They walk as I fly, far and long. There are mountains to the south of here, and mountains to the north. They came from there, walking, stopping to take what they chose along the way.*

A chilly little wind slipped between the leaves, touching me, leaving me cold for a moment. So we had a kind of dog that was willing to eat other dogs, who could travel for days and days, just stopping to kill food along the way? And sometimes the dog might not even really look like a dog?

Another voice popped into my head. This time it

was one of the two Cores sitting on the bench: *She said the gardeners found parts of something the coyotes killed—might be a cat, or a skunk . . .*

What wouldn't they eat, if they ate skunks and other dogs? Memorie hadn't given me a solid answer to whether coyotes ate cats or not; it was one of the first things I'd asked her about them. Whether they did or not, Memorie hadn't made it sound as if the coyotes were the kind of animals you could bargain with. They sounded like the kind of predator that took whatever it wanted, and kept going.

It was crazy. If they were here, in the park, they were going to ruin things for all of us. We had a balance that kept us all alive. If they just took what they wanted, they were going to rip that balance apart. And no matter how much I thought about it, I couldn't see any way of fixing the problem.

Even the long walk from our feeding spot to Memorie's tree hadn't managed to burn up all the dinner I ate, because I wasn't hungry enough to come out from the bush and try hunting. There wasn't any reason to do that anyway, not if the early-morning Warm was going to come by and feed us again. . . .

I dozed for a while, just resting. I was still getting used to the nights getting colder, and I could feel my own fur wanting to grow in thicker, denser, warmer. That hadn't happened when I lived with the People.

When I finally squeezed back out onto the path, the moon had come and gone. I stopped at the edge of the grass, washing one paw and then the other, looking around. There were no coyotes or anything else around, but I must have been sleeping deeper than I'd thought, because someone had come by, leaving a bundle of old rags on the grass just a few feet away, close enough to my sleeping spot to reach out and touch.

The rags sat up and gave a little chuckle.

"Well, looky-looky! What we got here? You be a cat. Hello, hey cat, daughter of Bastet, eater of mice, looky-looky-looky, hello there."

I jumped straight up. I was still edgy, wondering whether we could do anything about the coyotes, and the last thing in the world I was ready for was a pile of rags singing at me. Because it was that kind of voice: almost crooning a tune. Like I said, people can be very weird. You just never know. Besides, the pile hadn't really seemed big enough to be a person. Not noticing, not seeing—that scared me.

So I went up. When I came down, I was about three feet away from where I'd been, and facing the rags. My heart was going so fast, I could hear it in my own ears: *thumpy-thump.*

"Fly, kitty, fly!" The rags were moving now, pulling themselves into a pile of something that looked like a very small person. "Let the wind be helping you. You fly, and I'll tell you stories about your mama, okay? Yes, yes, yes? Hey! The cat's being the same color I'm being!"

She was very small and very black, and maybe old. I couldn't really tell. Her voice was like Memorie's, sort of; it wasn't as spooky, maybe because she didn't have the wind effect going on—her voice was grounded somehow. I could tell, as soon as she opened her mouth and told me to fly that she was never going to be able to fly herself. She was part of the ground, and she was destined to stay there. I wondered if that was why she wanted me to fly, because she never could.

"I can't fly." I heard myself answer her. "I'm a cat."

Now, that was just stupid. I can't communicate

with people—all they seem to hear is some version of *meow*. Some of them, the ones who like cats, can tell what my mood is from the way I make the noise. And if they really love cats, they can sometimes hear when we let them know our names—the Warms had known right away that my name was Dark. Mostly, though, cats and humans just don't speak the same language.

So I really wasn't expecting what happened next; it was so strange, it took me a couple of seconds to realize what was happening. But she straightened her neck, gave me a long stare, and suddenly grinned.

"I know that, cat." She was speaking People, whatever it is the People call the usual language. "Got eyes, don't I? But you could at least try. What you doing out here?"

"Nothing much. I went to visit an owl with my raccoon friend Rattail, and I stopped to think." It was sinking in, sort of sideways in my brain: *What, she understands me, not just the mood? She understands the actual words? How . . . ?*

"A raccoon and an owl? You went talkin' to Memorie, cat?" Her voice was still singsong, but I was beginning to make sense of it. She had moods in her voice, same as I do, and to my ears, when she asked the question, she sounded more *there* somehow. "What's a cat got to discuss with the Eyes That Fly?"

She waved her arms, and some stuff fell out of her sleeves—it was old newspaper. I wondered if she'd stuffed that in there to keep her warm, or to make whatever she slept on feel softer, or maybe both.

"Well, I'm new out here. And my friend told me Memorie could answer some questions."

"What kind of questions a cat need to ask Miss Memorie?"

"About the coyotes," I told her. "Have you seen them—I'm sorry, I don't know your name. Mine's Dark."

"You got a fine name there, Dark. My name's Sal. Preacher named me Sarey Anne, when he stuck my head in the water, but I been Sal ever since, and most days, I be Streetwise Sal. I saw you out here, maybe a week gone now, watching the foxes. You sit a little while, and I tell you all about Bastet, sing you a song from the Queen of Cats. How about that?"

I didn't know what a preacher was, or why he'd

try to drown her. But Sal seemed friendly enough, maybe just a little crazy in a good way. And anyway, we understood each other. "Nice to meet you. Listen, I should get back over to our feeding spot. There's supposed to be a woman who comes around early, and I don't want to miss a chance for breakfast."

"Now that's some sense. The black cat ain't no fool." She nodded at me. "You go on back, make a little room in your stomach—you ain't hungry now, but you will be later. And be nice to the foxes when you see them. They ain't got long now."

I'd already turned to go, but that stopped me. She sounded, I don't know, sort of sad and distant. Different. "What? What do you—?"

I stopped. She was gone, rags and all.

I sat there for a minute, wondering if I was awake, or if I'd dreamt it. I went back to the bush, where she'd been sitting. The grass was damp with the park's fog, but not as damp where she'd been sitting. And the grass there was flattened out.

So she'd been real, and there. But she was also gone, a lot faster than she should have been.

There are ghosts here. Some animal, some human.

Memorie's voice was loud in my mind. *One in partic-ular, both, perhaps neither—I am never sure which.*

I headed back for 'Blanca's bench.

The park sprinklers had come on, sending rivers along the sidewalks and into the street. There were hardly any cars out on the road, but the ones that did come by splashed up short walls of water.

I dodged the puddles, stayed away from the sprin-klers, and kept going. Casablanca hadn't told me when during the morning the Warm came by.

North across JFK Drive, through the big open meadow. There were shapes up at the bench moving around. Raccoons? No, the tails were all wrong and they didn't move like raccoons. What . . . ?

I was right at the foot of the path when I realized what I was looking at, and stopped.

Fox kits, four of them. From the looks of it, I hadn't missed breakfast—the babies were polishing off the dregs of our dinner. They weren't much bigger than I was.

On the path just a few feet away from me, some-thing barked. It was a short little bark, not a howl or a wail. It sounded as if something was coughing.

Okay, Dark. It's okay. Just back away, nice and slow. Let them see you aren't any danger to the babies. Then convince them you aren't breakfast for their mother and father. Come on, go.

I backed up to a safer distance. No one seemed to be chasing me; I risked turning my head and looked up the path.

The Red Father was watching me, nice and steady. Our eyes locked for a moment, my green to his gold. I thought I saw him nod, just a little twitch, acknowledging that he knew that my backup meant I was no threat to the kits. They weren't friendly eyes, but they weren't mean or aggressive, either. I was safe, for now.

His mate, a vixen who looked as if she'd been nursing the kits too long, stood at his side. She lifted her head and coughed again: the alarm bark, letting her babies know to be careful, stranger close by.

I backed away a few more feet. I must have looked pretty funny, since I was staying very close to the ground and keeping my eyes on the adults the whole time. The babies were no threat—they were too busy eating. And the Red Father made it clear that I was okay, if I stayed away from the food and the family.

Five feet, six feet, seven, and then I was away from the path and heading for a tree, as the morning sky got lighter around me. There was no sign of Casablanca yet. None of the Red Father's family had followed or chased me.

I curled up, hearing the soft patter of the kits as they finished the leftovers and followed their parents through the trees and away. And all the time, waiting for Casablanca and breakfast, I was hearing Sal's voice in my head:

And be nice to the foxes when you see them. They ain't got long now.

CHAPTER FIVE

Two nights later was the night of the shopping-cart fire and the police action.

San Francisco is a cold place. It's not as cold as some of the places Memorie told us about, sharing stories of when she was an owlet far to the north. Still, it gets chilly, especially when the fog begins creeping in, covering the grass, hiding the tops of things, making the lights on the buildings outside the park look distant and diffused. And in winter, when the rains come, it can get really miserable.

Casablanca had warned me about that, but I already knew; I had spent three winters—before the People brought their child home—curled up in my window seat, warm and dry as rain lashed the

windows and the wind off the ocean came up, tip-
ping the trees across the street to one side or the
other. This was going to be my first winter outside,
in the eye of the rainy season. I was already wondering how the best way to get through it was. To tell
the truth, I was scared.

The night of the shopping cart, though, we were
still in the time that comes just before the rains:
shorter days, longer nights, and the fog was getting
heavier. That isn't a bad thing, because the night is
my time, and Rattail's, too. I'm okay with the night.

But since I'd let the Warms at Casablanca's spot
see me a couple of days ago, I was hunting less and
less. The night of the fire and the police, when it
came time for food, I'd hung back in the shadows
and heard them. And it amazed me, really, because
they were calling me. They were worrying that I
wasn't there: *Jack, is that little black queen anywhere?* Dark! *Here, kitty. Hi, Casablanca, come and
eat. Where's your friend?*

There it was, thinking about it, that little disturbance in me. I pushed it away. This was the drawback
to being around people, the tradeoff: not having to

hunt, knowing where and when food would be put out for me, that came with being made to remember things I couldn't afford to remember right now: times when there was someone to call me to dinner, to worry about me if I stayed away, to use that coaxing tone of voice.

I'm not stupid. It was obvious the Warms cared about us, and there was no point in hanging back in the blackness, not if they were going to feed me. So I'd stepped forward and spoken—*I'm here!*—and Angie made a pleased noise. She fussed over me and set out food for me, and fussed over me some more.

I decided right then that I was going to mark them as territory. It didn't mean I was trusting them yet, not all the way, but there was no harm in marking them. I told myself, okay, and I gave the woman a head-butt, right against the ankle, and rubbed the scent-maker in my cheek against her. There's a particular noise a genuine Warm makes, someone who loves cats. When I did that, she made it.

Rattail came crashing up through the bushes a couple of minutes later, and while Casablanca and I finished our dinner, he sat up on his hind legs,

chattering and looking worried and playing up to
Jack and Angie. It was a show he put on for them, and
we all knew it, even the people.

Rattail settled down, sitting on his haunches and
tucked into his own pile; he caught my eye, then
Casablanca's, and gave us each a tiny wink. A water
bowl would have been handy, especially for Rattail,
but it wouldn't have lasted the night, not with the
Cores around. They're scavengers. Anything they find
that they can use goes with them when they move
on, even a disposable plastic water bowl. Besides, the
park sprinklers leave pools of standing water for all of
us to drink. Maybe the Warms knew all that, because
they didn't bother with bowls.

The Warms hung around a few minutes that night,
so we got to eat all we wanted without having to worry
about foxes. Eventually, they drove off, and Ratty and
I said good night to Casablanca and wandered off into
the park.

Rattail was edgy, and I wasn't sure why. He'd
stop every few feet, rear up, look around, come back
down, keep moving. Then he'd start the whole process again.

"What's wrong with you? You're jumping around all over the place tonight. What's the matter, Ratty?"

"Nothing." He spoke over his shoulder, and he was lying. He must have seen that I knew it, too. "I mean, I don't know. I'm not sure."

I sat down and began washing my face, licking one paw, drawing it back over my fur. "Well, how about slowing down? If there actually is something wrong up ahead, we might as well take it slow. Besides, do you really want to turn a corner at high speed and slam into something? Because I know—hey!"

It came out of the fog, careening down the path at us out of nowhere, bouncing from side to side as it went: a shopping cart, heaped high with stuff I couldn't see but which looked vaguely like the kind of things a Core might collect—old clothes, newspapers, rags. I thought I saw an old beat-up shoe sticking out of the top. The cart was on fire, and it was coming right at us.

Rattail let loose with one high-pitched chattery shriek and leaped for the trees. I was right behind him.

There we were, halfway up a tree, holding on for dear life and staring to the east with our eyes wide enough to be owls, swiveling our heads to watch. The shopping cart hit a curve while its wheels were straight, bounced, and went flying out into the middle of the road. It fell over on its side—we could hear it, a nice muffled *whump!*—and lay there, flames shooting out of it. From somewhere to the west, I could just pick up the sound of people laughing and yelling.

"Wow." I craned my neck and stared at Rattail. He wasn't looking at me—he was craning all the way around and beyond me, out toward where all the noise was coming from. Out in the middle of the road, the shopping cart was still burning. "What was *that* about?"

"Shhh." He was very still, concentrating, and I went still along with him. "Police cars coming. Listen—can you hear? There are sirens."

He was right. They sounded very weird in the fog, almost alive: a high-pitched rhythmic wailing noise—*DEE-you, DEE-you*—over and over. I couldn't tell which direction the police cars were coming from. Fog has a very distorting effect on sound—it muffles things.

They shot past us just a few seconds later, going east

to west, three police cars one right after the other with the red-and-blue blinking lights on top just flashing away, skirting the shopping cart and leaving it there to burn. *DEE-you, DEE-you*—loud enough to be annoying because they were right in front of us, but they were moving fast, and before I could even twitch my ears to try and filter out the noise they were making, they were gone, red taillights disappearing west into the fog.

"Whoooeee!" Rattail was already climbing down. "Sounds like some of the Cores are getting cra-*azy*. Want to go see what this is all about?"

We headed off down along the path, under the bridge that crosses over JFK Drive. The sirens had stopped, but that was fine, because we didn't need the sound to let us know where the action was. We could see exactly where things were happening; the police cars had stopped their engines and stopped making noise, but all the red-and-blue lights on top of the cars were flashing away, down there in the blanket of mist. And we could hear people yelling, but there was no telling whether it was the police yelling, or whoever had launched the flaming shopping cart, or maybe both.

We weren't alone out there, either; quite a few heads were popping out of bushes and holes and treetops. I saw a couple of skunks, and a few more raccoons. Even the gophers had stuck their heads up in a few spots.

But my fur had lifted. It wasn't because of the wind, and it certainly wasn't because of the gophers. There was something else, something I couldn't quite see, a scent I couldn't quite identify . . .

"Look." Rattail's voice had dropped low. "Across the street, by the lake. It's the Red Father, checking out the action. Wonder where his family is?"

That explained it; I'd sensed the fox close by, or maybe smelled him and didn't notice. Red Father's tail was at point, shoulders still and quiet, strong black nostrils opening and closing as he tasted the night air. He seemed more concerned with the burning shopping cart than he did with the people, though—his head had turned to the east, and it stayed there.

"Hey, *wooooh-hoooo*! Hey, piggy-piggy, can't catch me! *Right here!* Can't catch me! Hahahaha-*wheeeee!*"

That got my attention. I jerked my head toward the flashing lights and felt a tremor as the ground seemed to move under me. There were some heavy things running around down the street, people thudding their feet, more people joining in, more voices, some of them loud and weird, some of them obviously cops.

"Crazy-bad." Rattail shook his head. "They took something, you bet—stuff that makes them do things. Silly Cores. I wonder why they set their own stuff on fire and rolled it away? I wouldn't do that if I was a Core, or had stuff. Let's go see."

Even in the few weeks I'd been in the park, I'd already become amazed at the way people don't seem to see the rest of the world around them. That night was a good example. By the time Rattail and I made it down to the edge of the trees by Marx Meadow, there were already about twenty of us there. At least five cars went by, slowing down to stare at the cops and the Cores. Not one of them seemed to notice the rest of us.

What really got me, though, was the rabbit.

He was the first rabbit I'd seen in the park, and I couldn't for the life of me figure out how he hadn't been eaten yet, or what he was even doing here. He didn't look like anyone's cute fluffy thing with soft ears. The garden next door to the house where the People had lived, there had been a rabbit hutch in their garden, with little pet rabbits. They'd looked like stuffed toys, or blankets with feet. And they'd smelled like food.

Not this one, though. This was one big rabbit, way bigger than me. He was black, and white in patches, and he hulked. He looked hungry even though he was big, and he was mean looking, too—not something I would want to mess with—and he looked like he weighed more than I did. There wasn't anything little or cute or fluffy about him.

I nudged Rattail and nodded toward the rabbit. Ratty turned and jumped.

"Oh, wow!" He kept his chatter down to a whisper, but he didn't need to worry—a few naked crazy-bad Cores were running around and shrieking, the police chasing them all over the meadow across the street.

"What's a rabbit doing out here?" The rabbit turned and glared at me, and I had to fight back an urge to go hang out on the other side of Ratty, where the rabbit couldn't see me. He looked nearly as crazy as some of the people.

"It's the Bunker Bunny. I can't believe he's still alive! I thought he'd been eaten by now."

"The what?" The rabbit was alone, nothing and nobody near him. Everyone seemed to be giving him a wide berth and a lot of space, maybe out of respect. For some reason, that didn't surprise me. "What's a Bunker Bunny?"

"He's the Feral Rabbit. The one who got away." Rattail's head was jerking back and forth between watching the cops chase the crazy Cores and checking out the rabbit. "Memorie told us about him, remember?"

I did remember, now that I thought about it. Something Memorie had overheard, one of the dozens of small stories about survival in the park she'd shared with us the night we met: someone had dumped a litter of five baby rabbits in the park one night, near the Children's Playground and the big carousel. Some Warm had pulled into the parking lot there to feed the animals, seen the babies running all over the place and panicking, and tried a rescue. That was a good move, because baby bunnies are very tasty snacks, and they wouldn't have lasted the night—or shouldn't have, anyway. If I'd been out there then, I probably would have hunted a couple down myself.

According to Memorie, the Warm had managed to catch four of them. The fifth one got clean away, running off into the bushes and out the other side. It had become a park legend: the baby bunny who'd actually survived, going feral, living rough and mean, avoiding everyone and everything it could, and biting anyone who got close to it or tried to corner it.

Personally, I didn't blame it. I could sympathize with it wanting to bite things; there's something about not being wanted that makes you want to bite, and anyway, you have to be pretty cold to dump a helpless baby and tell it to fend for itself.

According to Memorie, the bunny only came out after dark, foraging for food, doing its thing, whatever its thing happened to be. Even the bigger hunters in the park, the hawks and the foxes, left it alone. That was something Memorie's stories had given me, the understanding that the park has a code, a set of unspoken rules. And one of the most important rules is that, if something's that much of a survivor, you respect its right to just be, and leave it alone.

"Right, I remember Memorie telling us about it. But why is it called the Bunker Bunny? What's that mean, anyway? What's 'bunker'? I don't know that word."

"I don't know either, not really." Rattail was getting bored with the action. "Want to head back? Maybe see if anything interesting is going on? There might be some leftovers in the Dumpsters, over by the carousel."

"Sure, let's go check it out. It looks like they're nearly done, anyway."

A few of the Cores had been caught. The police had locked their hands behind them so they couldn't hit anyone, and shoved them into the black-and-white cars. One of the cars had already pulled away with a couple of Cores in the backseat. One of the Cores was naked; I could see him through the car window. He was laughing and sticking out his tongue, making faces, but I couldn't tell whether it was at the whole world or the rest of the police—or if he'd seen there were animals and was sticking his tongue out at us.

The Bunker Bunny had already left, and so had most of the smaller onlookers. Two of the skunks were eyeing each other, tails flat—I didn't know whether that meant they were going to fight over something or breed, but either way, when a skunk puts the tail out like that, I'd rather be elsewhere.

Rattail and I headed out, moving east and away, leaving the crazy-bads and the police and the rest of the onlookers behind us in the fog.

We stopped for a couple of minutes by Rainbow Falls. It's a funny place; they're tall and majestic and totally fake. Nature didn't make them, and neither did time—people did. Someone in a building somewhere decides they want the Falls to be on, and water comes roaring down into a neat little lake. Sometimes the Cores use the Falls to take showers. I'd passed by a couple of times when that was happening—you could hear them swearing half a mile away in the dark. I guess the water was cold.

We hung out for a few minutes, resting, taking our time. I was scenting the air, tasting the different smells that hung in the mist like raindrops. Most of them were familiar, but there were one or two I couldn't put names to. . . .

"What are you doing?" Ratty was up on his hind

legs, looking around, kind of nervous. "Sniffing like that? Do you smell something bad?"

"Just trying to see what's been here, that's all. It's been pretty busy out here tonight." Skunk, possum, more skunk, car exhaust, dog, dog, human, raccoon, different dog—maybe it was Red Father . . . ?

Maybe not. All my fur was suddenly standing, and there it was, the desire to growl.

Warning, danger, something bad. I kept my voice low. Everything on me was stiff, and my shoulders had hunched up.

"Rattail. Do me a favor and concentrate for a minute. There's something out here, and I can't put a name to it. Close your eyes and take a breath. Are you getting anything? What do you smell?"

He ignored the part about closing his eyes. But he was sniffing, all right. He was very stiff himself, all of a sudden. "Something a little way to the east. Dog, maybe. Is that what you meant? That dog smell?"

"I think so. Maybe it's fox? I saw Red Father coming up this way a while ago—"

I stopped, biting off the words. Somewhere up the road, deep in the fog curling in under the trees, something had screamed. It was a bad noise, very bad—full of fear and pain.

We ran. We didn't talk, we just ran, turning and running up the road, and as we ran, I was using all my senses, feeling the dog-smell growing stronger as we got closer to—

"Rattail. Stop." I wasn't moving, not now. My claws had come out. "Something happened. Someone made a kill. I can smell the blood."

He skidded to a stop, a foot in front of me. His teeth were showing, and his nose was wrinkled up. I didn't even have to ask him if he'd caught the smell.

Raccoons don't smell as well as cats do. So whatever had happened, whatever blood had been spilled, there had to be a lot of it. And it had to be pretty close by, because he was getting it, too, that smell on the night air. It was rich and dark and coppery, and it woke up all the reactions in me: fear, hunger, the desire to hunt, to kill, find the blood, spill more of it . . .

We ducked back into the bushes and crouched, watching and waiting. A bicycle went by, a girl wobbling on the tiny seat; there was a red light flashing on the back, and I thought the bicycle looked like a silly copy of the police cars. . . .

It came out of the fog as if it were made of the night, loping along, heading toward the western reaches of the park, out where the ocean meets the land. It was a dog but not a dog, gray and red and pale, with thick fur, a long face, long ears. It wasn't even that big, not really—I'd seen people with their dogs, and they were larger than what was moving along the path in front of us now.

I couldn't tell you why I was so scared. I just knew I was. Somewhere in my head, I could hear Memorie: *You will know them when you see them, and when you see them, trust your muscles and be prepared to fly.*

I gathered my muscles. There was a tree behind me. Rattail knew what I was going to do—he was right there with me. This dog, and I'd already guessed what it had to be, had seriously spooked both of us. Just before I leaped for the tree, the dog turned and looked at us.

There was blood on its muzzle. There was blood on its chin.

I don't remember getting up the tree. I don't remember Rattail—who was chattering and hissing and right on the edge of that aggressive thing male raccoons do—getting up there, either. But there we were, looking down from a branch, all my muscles locked up hard and tight.

I knew what it was now, sure and certain. Memorie had told us what to look for, and this was it. Trickster.

The coyote found us with its eyes. They were a deep gold, the same color as Casablanca's and the foxes' eyes. But they were empty, cold as the change in the winter Ratty had warned me was coming. If there was anything in there to reach, it was locked hard and secret, somewhere behind those eyes. The eyes themselves were barred shut.

We were in trouble, and I knew it. Casablanca had called the coyote a scary-bad, and she was right about part of it. It wasn't bad—but it was scary.

The coyote didn't care about the park. It didn't care about how we balanced things, about how we all stayed alive. I saw it in that cold golden eye; it was clear to anything with any sense of self-preservation that there would be no compromises. The coyote didn't care. It would take what it wanted.

For just those few seconds, we stared down and it stared back up. Then the coyote loped off and was gone. As it went, I caught sight of a dark smear, what looked like an open wound on its flank, and a patch where the fur had been torn out.

We stayed in the tree a good long time. When we finally did come down, we followed the blood-smell northeast, staying as close to the deep cover of the bushes. Neither of us said one word. There was nothing to say, not then.

There were a few drops of blood on the path, and more on the grass. The smell got really strong as we came to the trees near the Rose Garden. I was growling under my breath, trying to stop it, trying not to let it out. The coyote-smell was weak, almost gone, but tonight, I wasn't willing to just trust my senses or my instinct. How did I know there weren't more of them? Didn't dogs—all dogs—travel in packs?

We turned the corner, edging around the quiet bushes full of flowers. We stopped, looking down. Next to me, I could hear Rattail breathing, heavy and hard.

I don't know whether the Red Father had died fighting or whether he'd been taken by surprise. Either way, he hadn't gone easily. The grass was gouged, speckled with torn, bloodied fur; some of it was fox, some not. There was very little left of him.

I stood looking down, remembering. What had Memorie said?

The coyote cares nothing for anything but itself and its young. It will destroy those who seek to compete or share with it. I would weep for all of you who dwell on hard ground, were I young enough to weep.

CHAPTER SIX

A few nights later, I ended up in the stupidest position you could possibly imagine: stuck in a Dumpster, hiding until a couple of Cores, mad and flipped out on something crazy-bad, went away. Not only stupid, it was dangerous, too. It could have easily ended up with me getting ripped to shreds.

If it had just been the Cores, it wouldn't have been any problem, because I could have slipped out the back of the Dumpster and headed up the nearest tree. But they had a dog, and I really didn't want to tangle with that one. I'd seen them before. I'd seen the dog, too.

I don't know what they'd been doing before they showed up at the Dumpster. I don't really understand why people do most of what they do—I just know they do it. Sometimes they are really angry and noisy.

Having to live out-of-doors all the time, having to sleep on a bench when they used to have blankets and walls and things, well, maybe that got to them. Maybe when you've spent years inside, only going outside when you feel like it, having nothing to breathe but the open air makes you crazy. It's not easy, not having any choices.

I don't like this time of year, because it hurts. There are too many things about this season that force me to realize that my own choices had become pretty limited.

It was late in the fall, close to winter, with the smell of cooking turkey lacing the air. I remembered that, from before the Dumping. There's something about the change of the seasons that affects how the people eat, and what they do with their food. It must be nice to be an omnivore, being willing to eat a lot of different things—you can change around all you want.

So the smells in the park, especially what was coming out of the Dumpsters, were poking at me, making me think back. The memories hurt as much as ever.

But for some reason, I didn't want to push them away as hard as I'd been doing for the first weeks outside.

So I was remembering, thanks to the Dumpsters. I was remembering how the house had smelled, just before the rains came. The rainy-season kitchen smelled a lot better, if you ask me, with turkey on the table, and the entire house holding a soft little breath of that scent on the air for days after. And they used to strip the meat off the bird bones and mix the scraps in with my cat food.

I think I must not have been adjusted to the change in the weather myself, because I slept too long and missed my chance at getting some wet cat food up at Casablanca's usual spot. I'd been sleepy, a little spacey, not wanting to concentrate or really move too much—there was a chill in the air that somehow made me sorry, as if the year was pulling in on itself like a pillbug, drawing away from me, leaving me stranded. It felt like there was nothing out there for me to keep.

I don't like change. And this change, the season, I reacted to that by sleeping a lot. That worked fine, up to a point; the problem was, when I woke up I was ravenous, my stomach making noise. But the moon had come up and was almost over the horizon again, and that meant me that I'd messed up and missed dinner. Jack and Angie would have been gone hours ago.

I cruised over to Casablanca's bench, but no luck. When I got there, the wet stuff was all gone. Plus, there were about ten raccoons, all in bad moods, squabbling and aggressive, ready to fight over a couple of little piles of dry kibble crumbs.

I headed across the street, sat down to groom, and thought it over. By this point, my stomach was growling louder than the raccoons had been. I tried to decide which of the two Dumpsters closest to Casablanca's to hit for a dive. One of them isn't too far away—just a few minutes to the west, near the road that goes up to Stowe Lake. The other Dumpster is behind the carousel, by the Children's Playground, to the east. The lake Dumpster is closer, but it has drawbacks to it—or at least, that's what I told myself; it was much darker, with deep tree cover behind it, and a log cabin that things could hide behind, watching you, waiting for a shot to take you down.

Besides, that Dumpster is too close for comfort to the rose gardens where we'd seen the coyote's carnage. The truth was, I couldn't push the memory of what the coyote had done to the Red Father out of my head. But I wasn't admitting that to myself.

So I opted for the playground and the carousel instead. Besides, the Dumpster at the carousel is a lot bigger, with higher sides. It gives a lot more shelter.

That looked like a smart choice at first. Not only was there no one else near it or in it, someone had tossed a lot of sandwich leftovers and chicken bones; I think there must have been a picnic out in the big meadow earlier that day.

I got deep into the Dumpster, nosing through papers and bottles and trash, following the smells all the way down. It was going to rain; I could smell the water in the air, moving in off the ocean. Some nights the fog is so thick, things just loom up out of nowhere. Those nights, there're pools of water on the ground in the morning, just from the fog. But that's a different thing from real rain. I can smell that with no trouble, and I was smelling it tonight.

I was hunkered inside the Dumpster, holding a

bone down with one paw while I wrestled scraps of meat and fried crumbs off it, when I suddenly heard voices, human voices. There were people coming down the path. I stiffened up, waiting, hoping they'd ignore the Dumpster and just keep walking.

I got half my wish, because they weren't interested in the Dumpster. Only half, though—they stopped right next to it. I was just about to grab another hunk of chicken and slip out the back when I heard a jangle of chain and a soft, low growl—the sound of something snuffling and panting—and I froze in place.

"Nightmare! Sit down, you stupid dog, don't make me kick your ass! Nothing in that Dumpster for you."

The voice was familiar, and so was the dog's name. It took only a moment for the scene to come back to me: the first night I'd caught a gopher, meeting Rattail, voices and the pad of paws, Rattail saying *tree, let's move, bad, crazy-bads, dangers, move it!* The smell of bad, coming off the boy in waves, and the dog, big and dark and cold.

I held very still, wishing I'd had the sense to just dive in, get my chicken bone, and get myself safe up a tree. *Go away,* I was thinking. *Go—just stay away*

*from the Dumpster. Go away, crazy-bads, and take
your big cold dog with you.*

The smell of them hadn't changed since that first
time. These weren't basic Cores, they were Dangers.
One of them was, at least.

The boy who'd called Nightmare by name, both
times, he sounded just as cold, just as raw-edged, as
he had the first time. I wonder how many of them
there were. If I had to outrun the dog, I might be in
trouble. "What are staring at me for? Don't give me
any crap and don't give me any of your *looks*, either.
Nightmare, I told you to sit down!"

There was no rustling of the dog's chain. Maybe
I could just stay in here until they moved away. At
least it was dry, so far; I could hear the light patter
of drops, the very first rain of the season, hitting the
paper bags and bottles at the top of the Dumpster,
small intense *splat* sounds. It was actually comfortable in there, compared to being outside and wet.
Maybe it would get wet enough to make them run for
cover, and I could just wait them out in here.

"Oh man, is it raining? Sucks. You been hearing
any of that talk going around, about the coyotes?"

All of a sudden, I wasn't comfortable and I wasn't wishing I was somewhere else, either. Information was out there.

I settled down, making no noise at all, and waited.

"Serious wimps." *Come on,* I thought, *keep talking. What about the coyotes? I need to know more.* "Crying like a little girl. It's just a couple of coyotes." He said it differently than I'd heard before: *ca-yoots.*

"Come on, Billy, that's major cold." That was the friend again, Jesse or something. From the sound of it, there were just the two of them, and the dog Nightmare. Maybe Jesse wasn't as scared of his friend as I was. "That girl whose puppy got picked off? If you woke up and saw Nightmare being ripped apart by a coyote, you'd freak out, too."

"You arguing with me, Jesse?" He sounded mean as a snake. "Or you just stupid? Give me a break. Any coyote gets next to Nightmare, the coyote better have his insurance paid up. Okay, okay, I get the girl being freaked. But you know that big camp up behind Strawberry Hill? I went through there last night and there were all these guys, man, they were talking about the coyotes and they were all freaked out. One of them said they got talking with some of those cat-feeder people. The feeders said there might be, like, ten coyotes in the park. These dudes were shivering in their shoes. Wimps."

I forced myself into quiet. It wasn't easy—everything in me wanted to tense and twitch. Ten coyotes? *Ten?*

"Sounds like they're breeding. Did they say what anyone's planning to do about it?" Jesse didn't seem as messed up as his friend, not as mean, not as angry. He was more just curious, the way a cat might be curious. And he was asking just what I needed to know. I found myself liking him a little bit.

"How should I know? And why do you care?"

"Well, they can't just let a lot of coyotes run loose in Golden Gate Park—someone's gonna get nailed, maybe get killed. I mean, yeah, okay, Nightmare tangles with a coyote and the coyote's meat. But some of the kids in the park, their dogs aren't like Nightmare. Smaller, not as good at fighting. One of them wakes up and finds their dog getting into it with a coyote, they're going to jump in and try to help their dog. If that happens, the kid's gonna lose an arm, maybe even get killed. Then someone else sues the city, there's stuff all over the papers, the kid's mommy comes out of the woodwork, does the whole *oh boo hoo my poor baby* dance, and puts the hurt on the city. All kinds of big bucks, dude. They can't afford it."

It was really raining now, water making noise against the trees above me and the Dumpster below. Good. As long as the noise didn't drown out the information about the coyotes, I was fine with it.

"Yeah, right, like I'm supposed to give a crap. You a law-school dropout or something, punk?"

"My father's a lawyer."

There was something about the way Jesse said that word *father*—I don't know. I couldn't tell whether it hurt or made him angry or what. I just knew there was a tone in there, louder than the rain if you had the ears to hear it. I wondered if maybe whatever was causing that tone was what had made Jesse prefer to live in the middle of a park in the first place.

"Yeah, your father, whatever. You wanna stop talking like *Law and Order*, maybe?"

"You're not thinking. Something like that goes down, we got TV and stuff, and what's the first thing the cops always do when someone twists their arms to do something? They sweep, that's what. They kick our butts out of the park."

"Shut up." Crazy-bad, crazy-mean. "You're a bummer, Jesse. Your lawyer daddy ever tell you that? Maybe when he tucked you in at night?"

"Whatever." If the words hurt, Jesse wasn't showing it. I wondered how old he was, how long he'd been out here, how long it took him to grow some scar tissue. "Man, I don't know about you, but it's raining too hard to hang out. I'm heading for some cover. You want to get your dog off that Dumpster?"

"Nightmare! Get off that thing, you moron. I said, *down!* You want into that thing so bad, maybe I'll just drop you in and leave you there, see how much you really want it. How about that for an idea? Leave you in the Dumpster like garbage? Dumb dog!"

I wasn't moving at all, not now; my fur was flat, my muscles were tensed and tight, and I was ready to jump. I'd felt the tiny shift of the Dumpster, heavy as it was, the weight of the dog as he got up on his hind legs and put his paws against the side. I could see him in my head, big and black and cold, smelling, wondering if he was really smelling cat, something he could find and chase and catch and kill and eat.

I risked a look up, through the old newspapers and garbage covering me. There were trees, plenty of them and easy to climb, but not close enough, or maybe they were. It depended how good a head start I could get, how much distance I could put between myself and the dog, how strong a jump I could get off the edge of the Dumpster, across the walkway, up the nearest tree . . .

Blip. DEE-you, DEE-you, blip.

I saw the police car's roof lights flashing just before I actually heard the siren. A car door slammed, very close by, and then there was a new people-voice, the kind of voice that didn't sound as if people would want to argue with it.

"You know it's after ten thirty, boys. There's a curfew in the park. Let's see some ID, both of you. And why isn't that dog on a leash?"

I hadn't known just how tight I was, how scared, until I let myself relax. When you relax your muscles and the difference is so much that you're shaking, you know you were tight.

I waited a long time after the voices and footsteps and car-engine noises were gone before I risked climbing out of the Dumpster. I was soaked to the skin, all my fur plastered against me. While I was down there hiding, the rain had settled down into a strong, steady downpour. It had soaked the Dumpster, leaving puddles on the bottom and making everything in it a soggy mess, including me.

I got out and headed up the path, trying to not get too close to the carousel. That thing seems very strange to me—it's big, and full of painted wooden animals that go up and down as the thing itself turns faster and faster and music plays. This isn't really my part of the park, but I'd spent one afternoon up a tree with Rattail. All these families had their kids with them. They settled them on different wooden animals, standing back and watching the children just go in circles. Some of the kids were happy; some of them—mostly the younger ones—were scared and yelling, holding out their arms and wanting to come down. All the grown people seemed to think everyone was happy. Very weird. I'd asked Rattail why they would want to do that. But he didn't know.

Whatever it's for, that thing gives me the creeps. I keep wondering if all those painted animals, the horses and swans and tigers, aren't actually real animals that were caught by something, trapped and captured, frozen inside those bright wooden bodies, desperate to get out. . . .

I don't know whether I heard it or saw it out of the corner of my eye. Maybe my nerves and senses were strung so high and tight after the Dumpster and the carousel that I would have picked up on anything, anywhere, within half a mile. Or maybe I hadn't smelled it before because the smell of wet Nightmare was so strong. I don't know.

I just know I veered suddenly, following some kind of little signal in my head that was like my very own personal *DEE-you* siren. I went hard and fast off to the south and up the nearest tree, clawing the wet bark and not thinking about anything at all until I was fifteen feet up a straight trunk and holding on to a branch for dear life. Panting and drenched, I peered down and around.

There were two figures in the pelting rain: a hunter, and what it was killing.

It wasn't the same coyote I'd seen before. I could tell that much. This one was smaller, concentrated. It seemed to have a lot more pale fur than the one

I'd seen. They'd been right about there being more than one.

The coyote had something in its jaws and under its paws. It really did look like a dog, the way it was built, the way it moved. It was actually beautiful, sleek the way dogs are when they're made streamlined and compact. And I thought, this is what Nightmare would have looked like, ripping me apart, if that police car hadn't come when it did.

I watched the coyote.

I was lucky there was nothing dangerous higher up in the tree, because I wasn't seeing or hearing anything but the coyote. I was concentrating on it completely. I saw where its muscles were, its strengths, where all the threats would come from. I saw its weaknesses. I watched it, and I learned it— what it was, what it could do, what it would do.

So I was concentrating hard on the coyote, and maybe that kept me from taking a closer look at its dinner. When I did, though, I stiffened up all over again.

It was the Bunker Bunny, at least most of the Bunker Bunny. Rabbit fur doesn't look quite the same when it's wet, especially when there's blood streaking it.

The coyote lifted its muzzle, keeping one paw on its dinner. It gave a little barking noise, very similar to what I'd seen the Red Father do that first time I'd seen him dancing.

Two young coyotes came out of the bushes where they'd been waiting, hardly more than pups, really. Babies.

That scared me, really bad. They must have been there, all three of them, the entire time the two Cores had been there. Nightmare the dog had sat there, with the coyotes close enough for him to have caught with one jump, and he hadn't even smelled them. It took seeing those coyote pups to make me understand that the coyotes had a lot more weapons than I'd thought.

I stayed in that tree, soaked to the skin, just watching as the coyote took the Bunker Bunny apart. She—the coyote was obviously female, the mother— reduced the Bunker Bunny to a smear on the ground. She wasn't just killing and eating dinner, she was teaching her babies how to kill and eat for themselves.

She showed them how to pull tufts of fur loose and throw them away. There was something, I don't know, tender about it—she was so careful to make sure they were getting it.

She stripped the dead bunny clean. And then she and the pups settled down, growling and happy, and ripped the stripped-naked rabbit apart into small pieces, the way I might eat a gopher. That rabbit had been bigger than I was.

I stayed where I was for the rest of the night, not coming down until daylight. Long after the coyote had led her pups off to wherever they had their lair, I stayed up the tree, thinking, waiting until morning before I felt safe enough to climb back down. During the night, the rain came and went, washing away the Bunker Bunny's blood, and most of the tufts of fur.

CHAPTER SEVEN

"Hey, Dark, pretty girl, where's Casablanca tonight, hmm? Jack, check out Dark! She's rubbing up against my legs! Jack, can you call Casablanca again—damn it, where is she . . . ?"

Angie and Jack were getting wet. I wasn't. I was under the long bench, and even though the bench was made up of slats, no rain was coming through. The food was staying dry, and so was I.

That was because as soon as the car stopped, Angie had taken a familiar-looking cardboard box out of the car. I remembered the name when she tore off a length of clear shiny stuff and stretched it tight over the slats in the bench, to protect me while I ate. Plastic wrap: that was it.

So Angie was standing there with the cat food, setting out our dinner. I was nice and dry, and Angie and Jack were both soaked through. It didn't seem to be bothering them much, though.

"Casablanca—here, kitty. She's probably curled up out of the rain somewhere. The afternoon crew fed the cats around five. I hate worrying about any of the cats, though. Especially since those boneheads over at Animal Control seem to be doing squat about the coyotes . . ."

I swallowed some wet food; if Angie was wondering how I liked it, I liked it plenty. It was a cold night, but the wet food was warm. I wondered how they got it that way, because it wasn't as if cars had ovens in them.

I stopped mid-bite. Another one of those memories caught me for just a moment: the People, giving me slivers of their food, always with the same phrase: *nice and hot, straight from the oven.* The oven had been a big box full of fire, basically. I didn't think the Warms could fit one in their car, though. How they were making my food warm was a mystery.

"Oh, good, there she is. Whew! Hi, Casablanca,

come and eat. That's right—is she limping? Angie, where did you put that plastic wrap? I want to put a little more over the bench—you missed a spot near the end of it. . . ."

"Hi." Casablanca settled down at her pile, next to mine. "Nice. I love warm food."

"So do I." I finished the last of my wet, and took a fast mouthful of the kibble. They'd covered the bench, but they couldn't do anything about the rain on the ground, and the piles of dry were soaking up water from the bottom up. "Is something wrong with your foot?"

"Leg." She was wolfing down her food, much faster than usual, and Jack must have noticed, because he went back and opened the car door. I realized that there were lots of cans lined up in a weird place, in front of the steering wheel, where the glass is. "Pulled a muscle. Had to get across the street fast. Stupid cars."

"Putting the cans on the defroster vents was a good idea." Angie popped the top on another can. "Wow, it's really starting to come down. I feel sorry for the people sleeping outdoors in this weather."

"Hey! Excuse me, but can you put that dog on a leash, please? We have feral cats feeding here."

That got my attention, all right. It had already got Casablanca's, and she'd jumped back and partway up the path. I heard a little noise from her, probably because she'd tweaked that sore leg, jumping.

I retreated up the hillside a little ways, not too far. No need to go far or fast or even up, not with the Warms standing there. No way would they let the dog get us.

"Oh, sorry. You bet." This was someone I hadn't seen before, a nice basic Blank, letting his dog run loose, not thinking, but not meaning any particular harm, either. "Jasper! Sit! Heel! Did you say you were feeding cats? You mean there are cats in Golden Gate Park?"

The dog was a decent size, but he wasn't huge, and he seemed to be pretty well trained, ready to do whatever he was told. He was sitting there, mellow and quiet, just hanging out with his leash attached to his collar. I glanced sideways at Casablanca and saw that she was thinking the same thing I was: the dog Jasper was sitting in a nice cold puddle.

"Of course there are cats." Angie's flashlight found us suddenly, and we both blinked. She sounded really angry, kind of fierce. "The black one's Dark, the tabby is Casablanca. There's also raccoons, possums, skunks, and who knows what else. There are even a couple of colonies of red foxes."

"Wow!" The man stared at us a moment. "Man, learn something new every day."

"We're standing in the middle of over a thousand acres." She was calming down. "How could anyone possibly think it was empty? Nature doesn't work that way. If there's an empty space, something fills it. And by the way, the leash laws don't say 'only until the sun goes down and you think no one can see you.' They're twenty-four/seven. This is one big reason why."

I looked sideways at Casablanca. She was in a crouch, waiting to see what would happen next.

"Oh, Jasper likes cats." The man with the dog rubbed its head, and the dog panted and waved its tail. I felt myself relax a little more—he'd come into the park as a Blank, him and the dog both, but I would have bet he'd be leaving as a Warm. "He wouldn't chase them, or even bother them. If my roommate wasn't allergic, I'd have one—I used to have two. Our neighbor's cat comes over the fence all the time, and they just hang out."

Jasper had seen us, and it seemed like the man was telling the truth; the dog looked interested, but that was all. He didn't look at us like he wanted to chase us, or anything. He looked, well, pleased.

"Maybe, but the cats don't know that." Jack sounded a lot less fierce than Angie, but that was no surprise; I'd already decided he was the calmer one. "They're scared."

"Under control." Casablanca headed back for the food piles. "More dinner."

"I'm really sorry. I didn't mean to scare anything or anyone—I'll keep him leashed from now on. Did you say there were skunks? And raccoons? That's amazing! I walk Jasper here about twice a week, and I've never seen a wild animal until tonight. Of course, I'm usually out a lot earlier. Do they mostly come out late?"

I followed Casablanca back down the hillside and settled down under the bench to eat. She was right: under control.

"Yeah, it's a whole different world out here after the sun goes down." Jack was rubbing the dog right behind the ears. "But thanks for understanding about the leash."

As if the dog knew what I was thinking, or understood what Jack had just said about us being scared, Jasper suddenly barked. Not a big noise—just a friendly little *wherf-wherf-wherfle, hey, hi there, how are you guys doing?* kind of noise. His tail was wagging faster now, splashing water from the puddle he was sitting in, and he had wet fur in his eyes bedraggling down from his forehead.

"Whoa!"

I must have jumped, because Casablanca turned for a second and just stared at me. She thought it was funny, me jumping—I could tell. That made me bristle, being laughed at; I swallowed another mouthful and spoke to Jasper. He really did look harmless, I thought, at least as far as dogs went.

"Hi. Is that true, that you don't chase cats? Or is your person just trying to make Jack and Angie feel better?"

"Nope." He actually had a neat voice, like a low,

happy bell. Big dogs sound like that sometimes. "No smoke. Cats are cool. The cat next door comes and visits once in a while—his name is Spike. I wouldn't chase him, or you, or anyone." He thought about it for a minute, and then corrected himself. "Okay, maybe squirrels. I might chase squirrels. But not cats."

Casablanca had finished eating, and she'd been listening in on our conversation. She groomed for a minute, and then walked up to the dog and sat down, and spoke to him.

"Jasper, huh?" The humans had all stopped talking, and were staring at the three of us. Casablanca ignored them. "Pleased to meet you. Name's Casablanca. This is Dark—we eat together, most nights. So who's the human? And where's your house?"

"Damn, how cute is that?" Angie glanced over at us. "They're talking to each other. I guess they must know your dog is okay with cats, somehow. Aren't animals amazing sometimes?"

"My guy? His name's Sam. And we live on Fulton, at Park Presidio." *Wherf-wherfle-woof.* "Why?"

"Used to live right near there." Casablanca stretched her legs and arched her back. The rain didn't seem to be bothering her much. "People moved away, left me. Still sleep in the garage sometimes; I've got a way in the new people don't know about yet. Dry in there. Lot of cars on Fulton, though. Have to be fast."

"I'm Jack, and this is my wife, Angie."

"Sam." He stuck out a hand. "So, you're out here a lot?"

"Nice to meet you." Jack put a hand out, and they shook. "Yep, we're out here pretty much every night, part of the TNR program the SPCA runs for the feral cats."

"TNR? I don't think I ever heard that one. What's it mean?"

"Trap, Neuter, Release. The idea is to catch the ferals, get them to the vet for spaying and neutering. The vet makes sure they're healthy and gives them the usual shots, and then we bring them back out here and let them go again. Dark just showed up a few weeks ago. . . . She and Casablanca are both house cats, I'd say. They definitely aren't ferals, anyway. They're much too used to people to be feral. Probably abandoned by their owners. And don't get me started on what I'd like to do to people who do that to their pets."

Sam rubbed Jasper's head. "I know what you mean. This one was a rescue, from a puppy mill. Jerks."

"Man oh man. I'm thinking the lightest penalties they hand out for animal abuse ought to at least involve drawing and quartering. . . ."

Everyone was standing around in the rain, both Warms chattering away to New Guy Sam, and Casablanca and Jasper talking to each other as if it wasn't cold and wet and miserable out there. I was wondering if I ought to try and make friends with the dog—weird idea—when I saw movement over the trees. Wings—big ones, wide ones—casting a shadow that was distorted and made scary by the rain and the clouds going across the moon.

"Excuse me." Cat and dog were meowing and woofing back and forth, exchanging information; they both stopped and looked at me for a moment. I was already moving. "I'll see you later. Nice to meet you, Jasper. I have to go."

The shadows on the path just behind the brightly lit street area were deep and dark. I slipped up under the trees and came out the other side. There's a nice little meadow down there, with a steep hill forming the eastern edge of it and trees and bushes along the top. If I'd gone up that hill and through the bushes, I would have been on a road that leads into the park from the north.

The other side of the road leads down to a big glass house full of strange plants called the Conservatory. I'd met the three cats that hung out up on the hill behind it. Two of them, Mask and her daughter Fancy, were locals, born in the park a long time ago. They'd recently hooked up with another dumped cat, a big orange boy who said his name was Pig. There was no sign of them right then, but they'd be out and around; from what I'd figured out by listening to Jack and Angie, the Flower Cats—that's what the Warms called them—were the last cats they fed on their way out of the park. So they'd be taking shelter and waiting for their dinner.

The rain had eased up, but the grass was wet and slick, and the ground underneath was a mess. There were gopher mounds turning into little pathetic clumps of mud all over the place. It was just as well I'd already eaten, because hunting in this weather would have meant a lot of work, and no fun at all. . . .

"Dark."

I stopped where I was. I'd been following the shadow of the wings, and that shadow was gone now, as the wings were tucked up and their owner settled.

"Dark. I am here."

It was a high voice calling my name, thin as the wind, moving across the grass, lifting all the fur on my back. I stiffened and raised my head, searching the sky and the thick mass of black-green on the hillside above me. As good as my night vision is, she was hidden away, even to me.

"Memorie?" I risked a harsher call and heard it carry, too long and too loud. "Are you here? Do you want me?"

"Memorie, yes. Words are needed. Look to the pine, cat, if you would find me. And keep your voice more to yourself, to bring nothing and no one down upon you, and so be surprised."

I found her easily enough after that; once I'd found the pine tree and placed her voice, she was visible to me. I went across the meadow and up the tree faster than I might have done another night. But there was something about what she'd said— *bring nothing and no one down upon you*—that had me taking care and moving good and quick. It also had me wondering what might be hanging out in the bushes, watching me, wondering if a black cat, on the small side but very fast and sturdy, might not be an easy grab for supper.

"You climb well, cat."

I'd settled down on a nice thick branch and was washing my tail, but that made me look up and stare. The owl's voice wasn't made to show emotion—the bird voice is high, thin, passionless—but I would have sworn I heard something in there, a shading or a tone: admiration maybe, or just surprise.

"Thanks." I gave the tail a few more passes and decided it was done; I'd picked up a lot of mud and small burrs and stickers from the wet bushes and high grass. "You won't mind if I wash while you talk, will you? I don't want to be rude or have you think I'm not paying attention, but the truth is, I hate having dirty feet. What's going on?"

"The coyotes have made a kill."

I stopped worrying about my dirty paw pads. The coyotes killing things, anything they wanted or at least anything they could catch—that wasn't news. I'd seen what they'd done to the Red Father. I'd been in the tree watching that mother coyote demolish the Bunker Bunny and use it as a way to teach her pups. If Memorie was bothering to tell me about a coyote kill, it had to be a pretty big deal.

"Are you talking about the Bunker Bunny? Because I know about that—I was there, watching from a tree. I told Rattail about that. He was really upset."

"No. But tell me this, cat—you understand the raccoon's distress?"

I was kind of glad it had come up, because honestly, Rattail's reaction had really puzzled me. It wasn't as if they were friends or anything. And things get eaten in the park all the time. "Not really. Do you know why, Memorie?"

"As I know most things."

Her ears were straight up, longer than mine, and her eyes were huge. Just then, she looked like one of the ghosts she'd warned me about, completely uncanny.

"Think on this a moment, Dark. The rabbit survived a dozen seasons, in a place where those of us who hunt at night could have taken him any evening we chose. Yet none of us chose to take him. He earned his life, his right to be left alone, his place in the park. He lived because none of us— not me, not the Red Father, not the cats or the dogs who live with the Cores or even the hawks and owls who give me first kill—none among us would have denied him his place."

I was quiet, thinking about it. It made sense. It was really simple, but it also amazed me that I hadn't realized it before Memorie told me: the hunters had all agreed to let the Bunker Bunny be. They could have taken him down anytime they decided that chasing a vole was too much work.

But they hadn't. They'd let him live, all except one. . . .

"Did the coyotes not care about what he'd earned? Or didn't they know?"

"Knowledge means nothing, not when the object sits square in the cold eye of their dominance. Rights mean nothing. There is no knowledge and no rights.

There are only obstacles to an end, and the end is to control, to feed, to sleep."

It was beginning to take on a very ugly shape in my mind. Not a pretty picture she was painting. If she was right, no one here was safe. . . .

She rotated her head, catching something on the night wind, some small thing moving far down below. "Had they known, it would have made no difference. They take what they choose. There is no wrong here, no blame. But it is what it is. This is how coyotes are, and this is how they live."

She was trying to get a point across to me; that was very obvious. But I couldn't help but wonder whether that point of hers was as simple as it felt. There are times when dealing with a creature as sideways in her conversation as Memorie was can be very tricky.

"You said they'd made a kill. Not the Bunker Bunny or the Red Father. Tell me, Memorie, please. Who?"

"A cat."

I heard the noise—a long, low snarl—and nearly fell out of the tree as it hit me: that was me making that noise, frightening myself with it.

We were stare to stare now, neither of us blinking.

"Memorie. Are you sure? Because the Warms—Jack and Angie—they didn't say anything about it. And they hate the coyotes."

"They said nothing because they knew nothing of it. The coyotes took a cat who lived behind the log cabin, near the road around the lake. The coyote—a young male, from the looks of it—came upon the cat three nights past. There was nothing left of it, save only a few scraps of fur." She watched me. "Near to your daytime resting place, and too close to where you feed, you and Casablanca and Rattail. Have a care to yourself, Dark, and say as much to those who share your space and your food. The coyotes are taking cats."

You couldn't have heard her voice through the rain pattering down again on the leaves over our heads. She spoke to me, and me only.

"The cat who was taken—his name was Charley. He was new to the park. We would have given him the time to find his own place among us, but the time and the turn of luck were against him. The coyotes took him. Charley would have heard the sound of hooves, and his choices were made too soon."

"Hooves?" I was cold inside. "Coyotes aren't buffalo or deer or something, Memorie. They're dogs. They have paws."

"Charley heard hooves." High as the wind, riding the night like a ray of moonlight. "The Bringer, the Taker. Charley's choices were all made for him. I have less fear for those raccoons who travel together, but soon there will be no foxes left here, and the coyotes are taking cats. Watch your back."

CHAPTER EIGHT

The morning after Memorie warned me that the coyotes were hunting cats, I went all over the park, looking for Rattail.

He hadn't shown up for dinner before Memorie called me. He hadn't come for breakfast, either—he or Casablanca. That had me worried, just a little. After all, Rattail was my best friend in the world right now, even more than Casablanca was. And he hadn't been there, even though I know how much he likes not having to look for food.

I didn't know whether coyotes would eat raccoons—I didn't think so. I've seen raccoons that were almost as big as the coyotes, and they have plenty of weapons to defend themselves with if they're attacked.

But Rattail was my friend, and I was worried. So of course I had to do something about it.

I went all over the park that day. I started off on my own ground, my own territory. I crossed JFK Drive and went south, crawling under wheelbarrows full of old wood and broken pipes where they were rebuilding the old aquarium, and squeezed under the long mesh fence around the new building site.

I called for him, trilling, testing the air, letting my voice carry. There was no answer, just some of the workmen, looking around to see where all the noise was coming from.

I went all the way back up the road and looked east, to the Children's Playground and the carousel. I checked everywhere. I balanced on the edges of Dumpsters, calling him. I went behind trees and under bushes. I waited for cars to go by, for breaks in the traffic, and I crossed the road to look on both sides. I stuck my nose into a lot of little lairs and hiding places I knew about; I even found a few I didn't know about, places that might be useful when it started raining really hard. But Rattail wasn't around, not anywhere. And even though I knew I was probably being silly, it was beginning to freak me out.

That morning, the sun had come back out, and there was a nice wind blowing. The standing pools of last night's rainwater on the sidewalks and in the road were drying up fast. I grabbed a long drink from a puddle, found myself a quiet little bush to rest under, and thought about what to do next.

I was worried, and it took me a minute to figure out why. I mean, it wasn't as if Rattail hadn't wandered off to do things for a couple of days before. For one thing, he had a girlfriend—a small fierce little raccoon called Prairie—and he'd get into really strange moods when he'd go away somewhere to be with her. I hadn't been worried then, not at all—I was sort of looking forward to seeing the kits when they were born, because raccoon babies are like little fat fuzzy pinecones with feet. Seriously. They're almost as cute as kittens.

But that was before Memorie told us about the coyotes, before I'd seen just what they could do in the way of hunting and killing, up close and personal. And I'd been worried, about everything and all of us, ever since.

I took a couple of minutes to groom, washing everything—paws and pads and face and all my fur—and picking the prickly little seedpods out of my tail. That was a waste of time, because I already knew I wasn't done hunting for him yet. The more I wandered, the more I was going to have to groom again, but it was habit—and anyway, it gave me a rest break and time to think things through and figure out where I was going to look next. Wherever I went, it was going to have to be out of my own comfort zone, and out of his. I'd already covered all that, and I hadn't found him.

Anything west of Rainbow Falls, where Rattail and I had watched the flaming shopping cart, was pretty much unknown territory to me. On the night of the Dumping, I'd actually come into the park through the western end, but after the first couple of days, I'd moved east. I think it had been watching the Red Father dancing in the moonlight that had made me want to be somewhere else—if there were entire families of foxes out there, it meant there were probably safer places for me to be.

Besides, the memory of the Dumping, of not knowing what the People were going to do—the woman crying and asking him if they shouldn't take me to some place called a shelter, the man saying no, they'd kill me there, me staring after the car, starting to run after it, not understanding why they would do that to me: all that was still right there waiting to pop into my eyes, if I let it. But I wasn't ready to let it, not yet, maybe not ever. The point was, I hadn't really come back out this way since.

There are open meadows west of the Falls, ridges and closely packed trees. It's very different from the eastern end—the west has all the big broad meadows and most of the hilly curves. I stayed on the north side of the road; the bushes are thicker there, with more cover.

Passing the spot where Rattail and I had watched the police chase the naked crazy-bad Cores around, I stopped suddenly. It was the weirdest thing, but just for a moment, I felt something: a cool breath at my back, a warning, a whisper, I didn't know what—I just knew all the fur along my spine ridged straight up, and I felt my tail puff out.

And then I had it. Memorie's voice was in my head: *There are ghosts here. Some animal, some human.*

One in particular, both, perhaps neither—I am never sure which.

That was it—I was feeling a ghost near me.

As soon as I let the memory of what she'd said through, I saw the ghost. There were two of them, actually, ghosts stepping clear and free of the shadow of remembering, becoming visible.

I'd stood here with Rattail, watching and listening, with the shopping cart flaming away in the foggy distance behind us. First there had been the Red Father, loping off toward the east and his own ending. And there had been the survivor, the Bunker Bunny, who shouldn't have made it through his first night alone in the park but who'd found his place and earned it against all the odds.

Out of nowhere, just for a moment, I saw them both.

Both were dead, both were gone. Both of them had fallen to the coyotes. But now both of them stood nearby—just shadows really, echoes of things that had been alive but weren't alive anymore—and I could see them, feel them, mourn for them and for the cat the coyotes had torn apart, the cat Charley that no one had even known was there.

I picked up my pace after that. I wasn't worried about the coyotes getting Rattail—I kept telling myself that—and anyway, it was sunlight and coyotes don't like that, but you know what? Seeing a ghost is an uncanny experience, and it makes you feel as if you're open to things you might not have been open to before.

Whether I was open to anything or not, I wanted to find Rattail. I was going to feel a whole lot better once I did.

I'd been walking for hours, and I was going to have to walk all the way back, whether I found Rattail or not. So I stopped again to rest, in the grove of flowers near the big lake. It's a little sunken island full of bright flowers, right in the middle of the road. The road curves around it, going in two different directions. You can see the stables, from the top edge of it.

Slithering through the bushes, I'd picked up a bunch more of those sticky seedpod things in my tail. Someone had dumped a pile of rags and newspapers down here, lost the contents of a shopping cart maybe, probably one of the Cores who didn't need them anymore. I'd just settled down and started picking them free, when the rags spoke up.

"You come to hear my Bastet song this time?"

"Sal!" My nerves were tingling. "Would you please stop doing that! And no, I didn't come for music."

"You got good reflexes, babycat. What you lookin' for, anyway? Because I sure can tell, you got something lost and you be hunting."

"My friend Rattail. He's a raccoon—I told you about him when I met you last time, remember? He didn't show up for supper last night, up at the other end of the park, and I got worried."

"Why you worrying about a raccoon? There ain't much out there want to mess with a grown coon, you know that?"

"Not too many things, that's true. But I think coyotes might. And he's my friend."

"Well, I ain't seen a raccoon since last night. I be keeping my eyes open, you think that helps. But I tell you something that maybe ease your mind a little bit: coyotes leave the coons alone, mostly. They want to take down the competition, and they don't see coons as no big threat to them. Besides, a healthy coon can give a healthy coyote a whole lot of grief, that coyote mess with it. Meantime, you sit a couple-three minutes and catch your breath. I tell you all about Bastet."

Her singsong was making me sleepy and mellow. A quick nap couldn't hurt; I'd been all over the park and everything was telling me to rest a few minutes before I went back to my usual turf. Maybe Rattail was back by now, wondering where I was. . . . "I know about Bastet—well, sort of, anyway. She was some kind of famous cat—I think."

She shook her head at me. Even in daylight, I couldn't really tell what she looked like, not past her face, because her head was wrapped in old rags. She was eyes and smile and mood, pretty much. "You think? Oh, for shame of not knowing your ancestors, you silly Dark cat, you. Bastet was your grand-mother. She was your queen, your god, all that good stuff. She come out of a city called Bubastis, where she had her bed and temples and all. How come you not be knowin' that? Everyone ought to know their own grandmother."

The wind was just a soft little touch down here

among the fallen leaves and flowers, as calm and quiet as a bed, or a grave. "No one ever told me. Tell me about Bastet, Sal, okay? I'm listening, I just need to rest my eyes for a minute. Then I need to get back out there and look for Ratty."

She expanded suddenly, seemed to get bigger, and her voice went there, too. It was very strange: she wasn't even moving, and it wasn't as if her voice was any louder than it had been. It was more in what she was saying. Maybe it was because it was interesting, or maybe because it was all about me and mine, or maybe she really told it well.

I kept my eyes closed, getting my energy back, feeling it come back up in me while Sal told me all about Bastet, the cat goddess, worshipped long ago and in a place whose name I'd never heard before. Sal told me about how Bastet had temples dedicated to her, statues of the Cat Mother touched in gold and rubbed with precious oils. There were high priest-esses, human women who danced and sang the kind of stories that she was singing to me now, women who kept the fires burning and the gold at the goddess's throat gleaming under dancing torchlight, bringing baskets of fish from a river called the Nile, laying them at Bastet's feet, begging the cat goddess for her protection from war and famine. . . .

Sal sang me stories. I had walked a good long way that day, and my legs loosened up, tucked in, relaxed, got their strength back.

When I opened my eyes again, the afternoon was almost gone. The air had a chill to it, a certain wetness that smelled like rain before morning. Night was moving in, blowing east off the water out near Ocean Beach. I remembered the first few nights, smelling smoke lacing through the wind at night; there were Cores and others out there, lighting fires at the waterline.

It was going to be full dark soon. And even though moving around in the park might be easier once the light of day had taken all the people and the cars with it, this wasn't my turf. I was going to have to make my way back, through a place with no real landmarks for me to use.

I'd wondered, when I woke up from my odd little nap, whether Sal would still be there, and there she was, tiny and dark, her own skin and the rags she was wearing helping her camouflage as night came in. She watched me as I gathered myself, stretched, and moved.

"Wow, I was dreaming of Bastet. But now I have to go. It's a long way back across the park to where I eat and sleep, and I still have to find Ratty. Thank you, Sal. Do you come to the east side of the park often?"

"I go all over the park, babycat, 'specially where I be needed. I might come up one of these nights, keep you some company." She tilted her head. "You wait one minute longer, Dark, and talk to me about the coyotes. You been seeing them?"

She pronounced it the same way the Danger had pronounced it: *ca-yoots*. That was creepy, but she wasn't really anything like crazy-bad Billy and his Nightmare dog, so I pushed it away and told her about the Bunker Bunny, the Red Father, and what Memorie had told me about Charley cat.

"I hear that." She'd stopped smiling, and her voice had lost all its music. "The coyotes, they be on the march out this way—they don't mess with me, don't mess with people. But I seen them hunting, Dark cat. Seen a pair of them, killed a whole family of foxes just a day or three ago—vixen, kits, all of them. Soon won't be a fox left out here."

That upset me. The picture Sal planted in my head, of the coyotes tearing apart the Red Father's mate and children, that got all the way into my head and wouldn't get out again. I didn't even stop to wonder why I was so sure that the foxes the coyotes had killed were the ones I'd seen the night Red Father had been dancing in the moonlight. I was, though. I just knew.

"You go back and find your friend." She was watching me, very steady. "And you watch your back, cat. Times be getting hard and bad out in the park, and winter's coming in and all. Maybe I come east and see you one night soon, but meantime, you find your friend and be thinking about how you be getting a ride on out of here, and who you be getting that ride with. Ride out—that might be the only way to keep on going. Watch out how you go, now. You don't want to be late for supper."

CHAPTER NINE

After all that fussing and walking and wondering whether the coyotes had caught Rattail no matter what Sal and Memorie told me, he turned up for supper with Casablanca, at the normal feeding place.

I got there earlier than usual, settling in to wait in my preferred spot, halfway up Casablanca's favorite tree. It wasn't that high off the ground; it grew sideways mostly, instead of straight up. But it was high enough for me to stay hidden from clumsy Blanks and nosy dogs and people on bicycles until the sun went down. And after that, it was high enough to keep me safe from things that couldn't climb.

I was still worrying about Rattail, but I didn't have all my attention on being worried. There was some part of my mind that just didn't want to let go of Sal and her stories.

The more I thought about it, the weirder that whole encounter seemed. I couldn't even guess how she came to know all those things, about Bastet and her city, about the priestesses who didn't do anything except care for Bastet's temples and bring her fish from the river and rub scented oils on statues of her. Wherever Sal had learned them, though, she was really good at telling them.

And that was another thing—she understood my language. I'd never met anyone like that before. People could be intuitive about it—the Warms were—but she wasn't just intuitive, she was good enough to tell me stories in my own language. And that was freaky-weird. In fact, Sal had been so good at telling those stories that I wondered if maybe she'd been telling them to other cats for a long time.

I remembered nights with the People, the woman telling stories to her child to make it stop crying and go to sleep. I'd be curled up on my pillow outside the child's door, never going inside, and the woman would be telling a story. It might be as true as anything ever could be, or it might be nonsense—something just coming out of her own head—but when she was telling the child, it came out smooth and even and almost like a song. Sal had been the same: she hadn't had to stop and think, when she told me. She'd just told.

So I waited in 'Blanca's tree, wondering about Sal, wondering about what she'd said about me getting a ride out of the park, wondering about the coyotes. I didn't know what we were supposed to be doing about any of it, but by the time I was all done wondering, I looked down and there was Casablanca, coming down the path from the Fulton Street side, coming north to south just as she did pretty much every night. And there was Rattail, waddling along right behind her.

I slithered down the tree, face-first. I was so relieved to see Rattail, I went over and butted him in the shoulder, good and hard. "Hey! I spent the whole day looking for you! I went all over the park. Where have you been?"

"My place." Casablanca sat down and examined her own paws. "Ugh. Mud. Rained last night. Ratty came over to see me, stayed until now. Dry. Plus, food."

"What? You mean, you slept in a house last night? Wow."

There was a car pulling up, Jack and Angie. I could recognize the sound of that particular engine. Most cars look alike, except for their headlights, but they sound different.

Rattail didn't seem to mind the head-butt—he butted me right back, light and friendly. "Not a house, a garage. There's a way in from the backyard, a grate over a hole, and all you have to do is push the grate to one side. It was nice and warm in there, and dry, too, and 'Blanca said I could stay, so I did. The people who live there now left their garbage can outside, and the wind blew the top off, so we had leftovers. Mmmm, leftovers. Oh, good, dinner's here."

"Hi, guys. Oh, great—the gang's all here! Okay, silly raccoon, back up and let me pour this, okay? Hi, Dark. Jack, did you see that? She let me scratch her behind the ears."

I'd been right earlier, about more rain coming; it started as we were halfway through our food, and out of nowhere, we were right in the middle of a rain band and it was pelting down hard. Jack got the roll of plastic wrap from the car and stretched it over the slats, trying to keep the rain out. Casablanca and Rattail backed away until he was done, but I stayed put. I don't have much reason to trust people anymore, but I'm not stupid, either. It was obvious that Jack and Angie had no intention of harming me; all they meant was kindness. They really were Warms.

By this time, Jack was soaked all the way through, and Angie had run back to the car for an umbrella to hold over both their heads. It was too late for that, though—Angie's hair was wet and dripping—but they didn't leave, just hung out under the umbrella, watching us eat.

"So, anyway, what's the news? You said you looked for me all over the park. Really? Where'd you go? How far away?"

I crunched a morsel of kibble. "All the way out near the buffalo paddock, that's where. And all the way back again. You know what, Ratty, you scared me. I got really worried. I kept thinking that maybe the coyotes got you, and I needed to make sure they hadn't. And Memorie told me something bad. I wanted to share."

"Oh, wow. Really? I'm sorry—didn't mean to make

you worry." He crunched, snorted, swallowed, and made a face. Angie was watching him, and she was laughing. "Hey, Dark, you know what? You should come with Casablanca some night when it's raining. Sleep indoors, where it's dry. I'll come, too."

For some reason, the idea made me tighten up, and I wasn't sure why. After all, the idea of sleeping somewhere that wasn't in a tree, out of the wind and not having to worry about the weather or the Dangers or anything—why would that bug me? It would be a nice change. But there was something about going inside again, especially inside someplace that wasn't mine and had never been mine, that made me nervous.

"Well, I don't know about that." I was trying to be polite. "I don't think I want to be inside again, not now. And anyway, it isn't my turf—Casablanca would have to invite me."

Casablanca had finished her pile of wet, taken just enough dry to make sure the Warms knew we liked it and should keep leaving it for us. She was washing up, doing her paws and face and behind her ears, staying under the covered bench. She stopped long enough to catch my eye, and I knew she got where I was coming from, the not wanting to be trapped, not wanting to intrude on another cat's space. We couldn't expect Rattail to get it—raccoons don't think like cats, and it would be really strange if they did—but she wanted me to know she did.

"Come. You're invited," she told me. "If you want to. Don't have to. But you could. Welcome."

"Hi, guys! Do you believe this crappy weather?"

I hadn't seen the dog Jasper and his owner coming down the path behind us, and I hadn't heard them, either. The rain had muffled everything, noise and smell both. That was worrisome, because if I couldn't hear what was coming up behind me, I was in bad trouble. I needed to be able to do that to stay alive.

But here they were, the man and the dog. Sam had an umbrella in one hand, and the dog Jasper, on a leash this time, was getting very wet. He didn't seem to mind very much. That was one relaxed dog.

"Hi, Sam, how you doing? Hey, Jasper—man oh man, buddy, you look like a big old drowned rat. That dog is seriously wet. Doesn't he get mad?"

"Hello, cats and raccoon, hello." Jasper shook

suddenly, a sharp ripple that started back at his tail and went straight on up through his head. It sent water flying everywhere, coming off ears, sides, legs, tail, underbelly. All of a sudden, the air right around us stopped smelling like wet leaves and started smelling like, well, wet dog. We all backed up, including the people—it's not a nice smell, worse than the skunks, even. "Nasty night. You have someplace dry to sleep until it stops?"

"Hey." Casablanca was well into grooming mode by now. "Dry? Sure. Back in the garage."

"Who, Jasper? Nah, he's mellow." Sam was standing under a big overhanging branch, and the top of his umbrella was getting a steady hard stream of water, really loud, plopping against the top. "Besides, he gets his revenge for being dragged out in the rain— he covers me in stinkwater. I was hoping I'd catch up to you guys tonight—I wanted to give you the heads-up about something. You remember that first time we talked, you told me about the coyotes?"

I went quiet. So did Casablanca and Rattail. The dog didn't seem to know why, but he had good manners, so he piped down and was quiet, too, waiting for whatever we were waiting for.

"Did you see one?" Angie looked and sounded very tense, so tense that I wondered if she'd spotted one herself.

"No, not yet. I guess if they're out there in the bushes, they see Jasper and they decide not to come out. Anyway, I got to thinking about it, so I went and talked to the community-liaison person over at the park police station. I asked her about the coyotes, what the cops think about it, did they even know about it?"

Casablanca had moved up close to me. Rattail was still eating, helping himself to some of the kibble that was left in my pile. He was listening, too.

"They know, all right. Everyone down there has an opinion about it—it sure opened my eyes." There was a new note in his voice now. "One guy said something about how we ought to feel honored that they came here, because the Native Americans worshipped them or something. He was totally 'ooh' and 'aah' about it. All woo-woo."

"Honored?" Casablanca had hissed it, and we all turned to look at her, except the people. They were too busy staring at each other. "What does that mean, that we should feel honored because coyotes came here and started killing everything else that lives here? Are they stupid? Are all people stupid? They want us to think that?"

"But then this cop came in." Sam was still talking. "I was getting ready to head back out, and this one cop parked his cruiser outside, and he came in just in time to hear the end of it. What a total jerk— really mean. He just started mouthing off, staring at everyone in there. This guy actually said he hoped the coyotes ate every cat in the park. But the general attitude seems to be that the coyotes are a disaster looking for someone to happen to."

"It's more than your basic disaster." Jack shifted his umbrella. "More along the lines of a lawsuit. Did you see that story in the paper yesterday, about how all of a sudden there's dozens of people calling Animal Control to report coyote sightings?"

"Yep, I saw it."

I was listening, trying to follow it and figure it out. I thought maybe Casablanca was wrong: people aren't all stupid. The Warms in the park weren't the only ones noticing. They weren't the only ones reacting, either. . . .

Jack sounded disgusted. "According to the woman in charge, everyone who called her is a paranoid idiot, and we should just shut up. I can't remember exactly how she put it, but it was something like, 'All you freaked-out people need to calm down, and Become As One with the coyotes.' And the paper? No opposing viewpoint anywhere in sight. I canceled my subscription over it, and you better believe I wrote to them and told them why."

"What does all that mean?" Rattail had moved up close to us. "What are they talking about? I don't understand."

"Shhh." I was listening, trying to make sense out of it. All the fur along my spine wanted to stand up and bristle.

Think like a human. That was what I needed to do, think like one of them. Then maybe I could figure out what they were talking about, and what they were going to do about it.

"But—"

"Wait, Rattail. Please?" *Think like a human.* "Wait, and let me listen. I'll explain when they're done."

"Okay."

Think like a human.

I was thinking as hard and fast as I could, but it was tricky. I knew about the police—they were the people who drove around in special cars with lights on top. They had the power to make other people do what they said. I didn't get why they could do it, I just knew they could, and that was what mattered.

But I didn't know who the Animal Controls were. And I really hadn't liked the sound of that one man who wanted the coyotes to kill us. Why would he want that? We hadn't done anything to him. . . .

Angie was loading empty cans into a plastic bag. "Oh, swell, you met Jerry, the crazy cat-hater cop? Skinny guy, wears a buzz cut? Jerry the Jerk. Isn't he a treat? We've banged heads with him before. Did he go into his 'the evil cats in the park ate all the song-birds' thing? Because they didn't, and we tried giving him the information where he could go look it up, but he's one of those. There's no arguing or reasoning with him, either—he just wants validation for his 'tude. Last time he stopped while we were feeding the cats down near the beach and gave us grief. But that woman at Animal Control, that really ticked me off."

"Coyotes?" Jasper suddenly piped up. "I heard some things about coyotes."

"This is one messy situation we've got here." Sam didn't sound relaxed anymore. "You know, this should be pretty simple. Coyotes are dogs. Isn't this woman the dogcatcher? Shouldn't she be out there catching dogs?"

"What?" I'd stopped listening to the Warms. I'd stopped trying to think like a human, which was a relief, because it was making my head want to explode, anyway. Rattail and Casablanca were also giving Jasper their full attention. "Jasper, what do you mean? Heard about it from who?"

"Well . . ." He settled down, the big tail waving behind him. "It's like this. See, some mornings we walk on the south side of the park. . . ."

He told us about it, and we listened. He was letting us know as fast as he could. That wasn't Jasper's style—he was slow and mellow in how he looked at things. But he knew as well as we did that at any moment now, Sam was going to decide that he wanted to keep walking, and that meant Jasper would be going right along with him.

It was funny, though. Sam started talking to the Warms. And he was telling them the same story Jasper was telling us. So we were getting the story in Dog, and then getting an echo in People. Totally bizarre.

". . . this big Dobie named Early. Not really mean, he just looks mean. But she lets him run around loose out there, and he isn't very good about coming back when she calls him. He's got her very well trained. So he's gone and stuck his nose into a lot of holes and corners out there on that side of the park. . . ."

"There's a woman with this big Doberman . . . takes it out for a run every day, over on Martin Luther King Drive. . . . She doesn't leash it, not unless she sees a cop coming her way. . . ."

"So I was talking with this Dobie, this Early, and he told me he'd sniffed out a den near one of the little lakes, and the lair has coyotes living in it—a whole family of them. He said the big ones growled at him, and he was going to start mixing it up with them, but then the woman called him and he decided to go. . . ."

". . . said the dog was acting really intense, that he went very stiff and was growling. Found a hole or something. I was talking to this woman and she said she wondered what might be living down there in that hole. No, this was over by Elk Glen Lake. She didn't think it was ducks, though—there were ducks all over the place and the dog was ignoring those. . . ."

". . . so Early said, yeah, he wasn't about to take that from some coyote, he's going to stick his nose wherever and whenever he felt like it, and if the coyotes wanted to mix it up with him, they could bring it, and stuff like that. He said next time he went over and they gave him attitude, he was going to call them on it. I'm just telling you what he said. I don't know why he talks like that, maybe she talks like that, the woman who walks him."

"So I guess if there's an upside to this, at least people know there's a problem. But we'll just have to wait and see what happens. Anyway, I'd better let Jasper do his thing before we both end up with pneumonia. Catch you later."

"Oops, gotta go." Jasper looked over his shoulder. "Bye."

The rain was really coming down hard now, and the wind had picked up, too. Up above, the trees were noisy, but I couldn't tell whether it was raccoons or the wind and rain, or maybe both. The leftover food was already soggy. I headed for cover, with Casablanca and Rattail right behind me.

We spent the rest of the night hunkered down against the weather, in the tree I'd found the night the Red Father had warned me off his kits. This one went high up and had more branches in the canopy to break the rainfall. It had thicker boughs, too, making deeper Vs against the trunk. In a tree like that, you can sleep deeper and feel safe doing it. You're less likely to fall.

Sometime during the night, I dreamed about a cat who was worshipped by humans, a cat who was a goddess in her very own city, a cat who'd never had to sleep halfway up a tree in the rain. I thought I heard Sal's voice in there somewhere.

But I dreamed about coyotes, too, about a pair of them with eyes that weren't cold, eyes that held things that had to do with living, instead of dying or killing. The coyotes in my dream that night were just a pair with babies they loved and wanted to protect. And somehow, in the middle of the dream, Sal's voice became Memorie's voice and that became Sam's voice, talking about a big dog sniffing at the bushes. . . .

I woke up at first light, opening both eyes and wanting to stretch. The treetops were quiet; the ground was showing puddles, still and undisturbed. The ground looked really far down from where I was. The rain had stopped, but there was fog drifting down and beginning to settle from the sky. The leaves were dripping—*splat*—against my fur.

Rattail was snoring, little grunting noises, flat on his belly with his front legs dangling over the edges of the branch. Casablanca was already awake, and she looked at me.

"Hey."

Her voice was very quiet. I thought maybe she didn't want to wake Rattail. I could have told her not to worry; when raccoons sleep, they sleep hard and deep. "Strange dreams last night," she told me. "You going to look for that lair?"

I didn't know how she knew I wanted to find that lair. I didn't know why I wanted to find it, either. And then, of course, I knew exactly what she'd been dreaming: the same things I'd been dreaming—

I couldn't figure out how she knew that, either. "Yes. Casablanca, do you know an old woman named Sal? She's one of the homeless people here, but I don't think she's one of the Cores. She's . . . a little different."

"I know her." She didn't seem surprised by the question, but then, Casablanca didn't usually show her feelings much. "Dreamed about her. Why?"

I slipped past her, and she made room for me. "Just curious. I'll see you guys later."

CHAPTER TEN

You know what's funny? The way we think we know stuff and then it turns out we don't.

The going was really slow that morning. When the ground gets muddy, the footing gets treacherous, and you have to pick your way between deep soft spots. So it took a while to get where I wanted to go. I'd got about halfway to Elk Glen Lake when I realized that all my muscles were telling me I should take a rest.

I'd been doing my usual thing: using the trails behind bushes and trees and things, staying off the main streets and paths, keeping out of sight. I thought about hunting up a snack; one good thing about the rain is that the gophers don't like it much, either. It floods all their holes, so they were busy digging out new tunnels. Grabbing one of those would have been easy. All I would really have needed to do was to follow the vibrations under my feet and see where the little wet piles were flying up from. Wherever those were, there were gophers.

But they were out in the open meadows mostly, and hunting them would have meant trading the safety of the thicker bushes for the chance at a snack. Anyway, the vibrations under the ground weren't as clear during the day as they were at night, not with kids running around and cars going nonstop. I decided I wasn't hungry enough for it to be worth it.

So there I was, sitting on a patch of dry ground under a really big tree. I'd washed the mud from my legs and was just beginning on my face, when I got a shock that nearly sent me out of my fur.

"Hey there, kitty." It was a human voice, male, coming from the tree, and it was familiar. "You're in a strange part of the park—for you, anyway."

I moved, good and fast. Even as I was jumping and hearing myself hiss, there was a voice in my head saying, *No, it's okay, this is going to be okay.* I wasn't too sure how I knew that—I mean, it wasn't as if I was associating that particular voice with anything good. But I did know it. And I knew the voice.

It was the kid named Jesse. He was sitting on the other side of the tree, and was craning around it. He seemed to be alone—no crazy friends or scary-bad dogs in sight. "Nice jump. Not the best time of day to hunt. You want some of my sandwich?"

This was the first time I'd ever seen him in daylight. The other times, it had been at night, with his Danger friend and the dog Nightmare. I remembered that he hadn't been scared of his friend. I remembered, too, that something had happened to his voice when he said "father."

He tossed a piece of his sandwich in my direction, far enough away from him so that I could get it and still feel okay about it, safe about it. "Here you go. It's roast beef. Or would you rather hunt for gophers?"

I chewed and swallowed; definitely roast beef, lean and red in the middle. There was a smear of something on one corner, something that reminded me of eggs. I'd tasted it before, when a visitor at the People's had slipped me some of her tuna fish under the table. Mayonnaise, that was it. "No, sandwiches are better than gophers in the daytime. Good meat. Thank you."

That was ridiculous, me saying "thank you," because of course there was no way this kid Jesse could understand me. Different languages all the way.

"You're welcome." He stretched out his legs, taking another bite, watching me. "You're a ways from your usual turf, kitty. Don't you hang out over on JFK Drive, with that tabby cat and the bald-butt raccoon?"

"Usually." This was getting silly. He was asking questions, and I was answering, but I couldn't tell if we were actually understanding each other or not. Only one way to find out. "Hey, where's your crazy-bad friend and his scary dog?"

"Billy and Nightmare?" He didn't sound as if he cared much, one way or the other. "Elsewhere. I can't hang with Billy too much—the guy's totally loco. The cops threw him out of the park a few days ago, but he'll be back. Nightmare's okay, considering what he has to put up with. He just shuts up a lot and doesn't give Billy any reason to mess him up."

He understood me, all right. So that was two people who spoke my language: Jesse the Lawyer's Kid, and

Sal the Bag of Rags. And Jesse wasn't sounding like a Danger or a Crazy-Bad, at least not out here in the sunshine.

He tossed me another piece of roast beef. "So what brings you out to this part of the park, cat? And what's your name, anyway? Don't want to keep calling you 'cat.' That's rude."

"My name's Dark. And you're Jesse, right? I heard your crazy-bad friend call you that. Thanks for sharing your lunch with me, by the way. I didn't want to have to dig out a gopher, not with all these people and cars and stuff. Hunting under the sun is a pain in the butt."

"No problem. So tell why you came out this far in the middle of the afternoon. Did you lose something?"

"Not really. I heard a story from a friend of mine last night, a dog named Jasper, about some woman who lets her Doberman run loose. Jasper told me the Doberman found a coyote lair out here."

He was watching me, and it was tricky, figuring out the look on his face, what he was thinking. "Okay, wait a minute. I'm confused. You're looking for a coyote lair? Why? I mean, what are you going to do about it if you find it? You know coyotes eat cats, right? Shoot, they'll pretty much eat anything. They'll eat your shoes, if you give them half a chance. I don't speak their language, but I know that much."

That stopped me cold. The truth was, I hadn't even stopped to ask myself that. I thought about it now, for a minute or two. Something had sent me out here. I was pretty sure I needed to find that lair.

Jesse was right, though. Even if I found it, was there anything I could do about it?

I wasn't about to go sticking my nose down any holes with coyotes in them, that was for sure. But as soon as Jasper and Sam had told us about the dog Early and the lair, I'd gone right out looking, just going on instinct and a kind of pounding in my head that was like a voice with no words. It was telling me to learn everything I could, find out about it, know as much as I could.

"Dark?" Jesse was still there, waiting for an answer to his question. "What's your plan?"

"I don't have one. It's just that right now, I want to know where they are."

"So that you know where not to be?" He nodded. "Makes sense to me. Knowing what not to do is just as important as knowing what to do. You used to live with people, didn't you? You had a home. You're not a feral, you're a stray."

"Feral? Stray? I don't know what either of those things are." It was amazing how much he seemed to understand about me. It was like I was made of glass, transparent, like there wasn't enough rain streaking down to hide my secrets. "But yes, I did live with people. They dumped me because I made their baby sick or something."

"Allergies, probably. Sucks. They could have taken you to the shelter—they don't kill animals there, not in San Francisco." He cracked his knuckles and got up. "You want some help finding that lair? I'd heard that rumor already—the word's been out here for a few days, that there's a breeding pair with their pups holed up over near Elk Glen Lake. Want me to carry you? My cat at home hated getting her feet in the mud."

If anyone had told me, right up to about ten seconds before Jesse offered to carry me, that I might be nuts enough to say yes, I would have said they were nuts themselves. So it was a pretty big shock to find that I'd sprung from the ground to his chest, making him stagger. I didn't even think, I just jumped. It was about the last thing in the world I expected to do.

I hadn't let anyone pick me up since the Dumping. Trusting people wasn't something I was feeling good about, not these days. If Angie or Jack had tried it, I probably wouldn't have let them—the instinct would have been to jump away. They could stroke me and they could feed me, but I wasn't about to trust any of them enough to let them hold me. I just wasn't ready.

And yet? There I was.

I fit my body up against his jacket, feeling him curl one arm under my back feet, putting the other hand across my shoulders so that I could settle. It's exactly how I like to be carried if I agree to be carried at all, and it looked as if he'd been telling the truth about having a cat at home. People who don't have history with me and mine never seem to know how to carry us.

"You doing okay?" He had a good walk; I could feel it all through my muscles and my fur. I can tell a lot from how anyone walks—and not just people, either. He didn't wobble or weave around. It was a nice, easy way of moving, one foot in front of the other, almost graceful, and as sure-footed as I was.

"Yep." We were crossing the street now, going north to south, and I was laid back enough that I wouldn't stress over it. Instead, I was trying to separate all the different smells I was getting off his coat. It was a funny mix of stuff; some of it I could recognize, but some of it I really had to think about.

Soap was definitely there; his T-shirt and jacket had been washed recently. They were clean, and so was he. There was a tiny hint of wet dog, very faint and faded, and I suddenly got this picture in my head of the dog Nightmare wanting to play and being too freaked out by Billy to want to play with him. And there was a breath of the park itself on Jesse's clothes and skin.

But really, the thing I caught most was just, well, him. It was a little bit sweet and a little bit peppery, and it just smelled safe. It took me a minute to understand that the sense of safety was because he smelled partly like a person and partly like a blanket.

I started to purr.

Now, that really did surprise me. But there I was, being carried by a human so that I wouldn't have to get my feet muddy. I had both eyes open, and all of a sudden I had this feeling: I was Bastet, goddess, being carried around my city of Bubastis. Jesse was my servant and my protector, one of the priests in my temple.

And no one was going to screw with me, no one and nothing. Fifty coyotes could come out of fifty lairs and they wouldn't be able to touch me. I was Bastet the Mother Cat Goddess and I had a ride, and a protector, and he wasn't a crazy-bad Danger at all— he was a Warm.

"Heh." He had a good laugh, not too loud or rowdy, just a little snort that reminded me of Rattail. "That's one loud purr you have there, Dark. I get the feeling you don't get a shot at using it much these days."

"Not much, no." I was quiet. Letting him carry me was one thing, but that didn't mean I was willing to share all my stuff with him. And I didn't want to poke at the places that hurt, not right then. I wanted to enjoy the moment.

"We're almost there. That's Elk Glen Lake up ahead. And there's that fruitbat yuppie and her

Doberman. Hang on, Dark, and don't rip my skin off—it's under control. Hey! Bad dog! Sit, Early! Where did you get the idea that the leash laws in the park are optional, lady? I said, *sit!*"

I stayed where I was, tense and ready. But I wasn't going anywhere, not while I was with Jesse. I had this weird little flutter; I couldn't tell whether it was in my head or in my heart.

"Stop giving my dog orders! You don't own him." The woman was small and very skinny, and her voice was small and skinny, too: she sounded raspy, as if she smoked or yelled a lot.

What she didn't seem to have bothered noticing was that the dog had actually listened to Jesse and was obeying him. There were people all over the place, just enjoying the day and the lake, and the dog was ignoring the crowd and the woman, too. He was sitting there, next to the woman who was dumb enough to actually think she owned him, and he didn't care about a word she said. We'd locked up, eye to eye, and a funny thing was happening: I was winning the staring contest.

Jesse sounded bored. "Yeah, well, it's a dirty job but someone has to do it. Maybe if you'd actually bothered to take five minutes to train him, he'd give a crap about listening to you. Right now, he doesn't, believe me. Good dog. Stay down. No jumping on me. You got that?"

"Yeah, okay. No jumping on you—got it."

He was a big dog, Early was. But we'd been locked up in that stare-down, and I'd won it easily, and I suddenly got the reason why: he wasn't an alpha. He was big. He looked mean. And he could probably have bitten my head off with one motion of his jaws. But between the two of us, I was the alpha, the dominant one, not him. And he knew it, too. The stare-down ends when someone gives in and breaks the stare, and he did it first, not me. And that meant I didn't have to worry about Early, not now, not ever.

The woman was still shrilling away at Jesse, and Jesse was just standing there ignoring her, the same way the dog was ignoring her. I couldn't tell who was more contemptuous of her, Jesse or the Doberman.

"Hey, cat." He was very brown, with portions of him that looked almost black on his feet and ears. "Name's Early. You?"

"I'm Dark."

"You certainly are, but what's your name?" He winked at me, letting me know he got it, just a joke. "Pleased to make your acquaintance, Dark. You guys live in the park? I don't think I've seen you around before, at least not with Jesse."

"No, I don't live with Jesse—he's just giving me a ride today. I hang out up near the museum mostly."

"If you're going to tell me to put Early on a leash, maybe you should put one on that cat. If my dog takes a bite out of your cat, it'll be nobody's fault but your own." The woman had finally noticed the back-and-forth we were having, Early and me. Of course, she didn't seem to understand that we weren't fighting. Jesse did, but then, Jesse wasn't stupid. And boy, was she stupid. Put a leash on a cat?

I resettled myself in the cradle of Jesse's arm, and he automatically shifted his hold to accommodate me. The movement left my cheek and ear hard up against his chest for a moment. He was warm and solid, and besides the smells of soap and park, I suddenly had sound to go with it, the steady, solid *thump-thump* of his heartbeat. I turned my attention back to the dog.

"I was hoping to meet you, actually. Jasper—you know Jasper? He told me about you finding the coyote lair. He said it was near Elk Glen Lake. Was he right? Do you know where they are?"

Early turned his head and stared off toward the east. His mouth opened, and I watched him sniffing, nostrils tightening and then flaring. "Yeah, I know where they are. They're around right now. Bet you the whole family's home—the small ones are probably down the hole, but I'm getting a major whiff, so Mama and Poppa were probably out here not too long ago. Can't you smell them?"

I lifted my head, away from the steady reassuring thump of Jesse's heartbeat, away from the smells that were all safe and familiar. Early was right; they'd been here, or were close by. There was a coyote smell on the air. It was barely different from the regular dog smell, but it was enough to be obvious.

And it wasn't Early I was smelling, either. While I'd been trying to pin down where the smells were, the Doberman had moved off toward the dark green line where the grass met the denser bushes, nose to the ground, stiffening up, sniffing.

I craned my neck. The smell seemed to be getting stronger, but that didn't make any sense. Memorie had told me, and I'd seen for myself: coyotes don't come out in the daytime. They're night hunters. There had to be something in the wind, something they'd scent-marked earlier, something . . .

Out of nowhere, a dog howled.

It was the yell of an animal in pain. You can't mistake that for anything else, not if you've heard it before. Half a second later, the woman screamed, like an echo.

I jerked my head around, hard and fast, looking for Early. Before I could even focus my eyes on what was happening, everything went crazy.

I saw the coyotes first. They were both there, the pair of them, planted just outside of that bush line, facing the rest of us. They were big, scary-big; Memorie had told me that people didn't consider coyotes particularly large, but to me, rigid as a tree in Jesse's hold, they looked enormous. They were side by side, heads lowered. They were face-to-face with Early the Doberman, and they were both showing their teeth.

More than that—they really were tricksters. I'd

been looking that way just a moment ago and they hadn't been there. The whole place was full of people, and no one seemed to have seen them until just now, not if the way people were yelling and moving out of the way was anything to go by.

Early jumped back, away from the coyotes. There was a trail of bright red drops on the grass, coming from his right foreleg. The smaller of the two coyotes, probably the female, had a red stain on her teeth.

The woman was yelling, freaking out, losing it. She was making all kinds of noise from where she was, but where she was had to be twenty feet away from Early. She'd been so busy giving Jesse a hard time, she hadn't noticed her dog slipping off to go stir up some trouble with the coyotes. One thing she wasn't doing was making any move to get close enough to the coyotes to chase them away from her dog. "Early! My dog! Oh my God, someone help!"

The dog turned tail and came back to us. He was limping; it didn't look too bad, really—more messy than anything else—but the woman was still shriek- ing, and the handful of people who'd been nearby were all yelling and doing things with their cell phones, and there was all kinds of confused noise.

Early sat down hard, lifting his bitten leg and getting the weight off it. He was whimpering, sounding totally whipped and pathetic. I'd nailed it when I said he wasn't an alpha. He was all talk, all smoke, but no power behind it. "She bit me! Do you believe that? I don't believe that! She bit me!"

I wasn't feeling particularly sympathetic toward Early, if you want the truth. He'd told Jasper the coyotes had warned him off their babies, and he wasn't going to take that from them, because this part of the park was his turf.

So he'd thrown down the challenge and they'd thrown it right back at him, and he'd turned and ran. That's the first rule of being an alpha: you'd better be able to back it up, because talking won't put you in charge—or keep you there, either.

The coyotes were gone—I'd watched them lope off into the bushes while everyone was running around and yelling. I was relaxing, nice and slow. Jesse hadn't tensed a single muscle the whole time. I had that Bastet-moment feeling again: *My protector won't let anything touch me, no harm coming to me.* "Got too close to the kids, I'm guessing. You got what you asked for. You had to know they'd protect the babies. That's pretty messy, but I'll bet it's not as bad as it looks. Just a nip."

He glared at me, but if he was planning on doing anything past the glare, he missed his moment. The woman snapped the leash through the ring on his collar; Jesse said something about it being too little too late, but I wasn't really paying much attention. She hurried away, dragging the limping dog behind her. I was busy snuffing the air. The coyote smell tagging the air was faint again, a memory of itself.

"They go back down their hole?" Jesse sounded completely unconcerned.

"I think so. Well, now I know: there are coyotes here. One place I don't need to check out again."

"Nice to know you're smarter than Early is. Man, that's one dumb dog! Two against one, and he knew it going in, plus they're protecting babies? What an idiot. Still, hope he heals up okay. You all done here, Dark? Want me to drop you back on your own turf? I'm going that way anyway."

We headed back toward the museum, taking a shortcut over the hill, Jesse shifting me from one arm to the other to balance us better. It was a pretty quiet trip back—both of us seemed to be busy thinking.

"Here you go." He set me down on a quiet path, close to where the Warms fed us every night. "Catch you later. And Dark?"

I looked up at him, stopping in mid-stretch, letting the claw-sharpening I had in mind wait. "What?"

"I think things are about to get really interesting around here." He was poised to go. "Keep your ears open, okay? Not just your eyes and your nose. And watch your back."

CHAPTER ELEVEN

When something happens in Golden Gate Park, something that affects those of us who actually live there, the word gets out pretty quick: *Hey, did you hear about that crazy hunter guy with the BB gun? The one who shot the osprey out by the lake?* Or maybe: *The raccoons out at the western end said to be careful and keep your ears open, there's a gang of kids with motorcycles and they're riding careless and crazy-fast long after the sun goes down.* Sometimes, if the news is minor, it takes a couple of days to make the rounds.

But the news about what happened after Early got nailed by the two coyotes spread like a dry-season fire, raging completely out of control. Not only were we all talking about it, it turned out that even the Blanks in the park were discussing it. I guess that being where it all actually happened made it fresh in their mouths, or something.

When I say fast, I'm not exaggerating. I'd gone up my new favorite tree, right after Jesse dropped me off; I wanted to think, and I had a lot to think about. I'd had a lot of surprises that day, and I wanted some time to process them.

Jesse hadn't been gone more than an hour when I heard a screech of a car's brakes on the big street and the yell of a person out a car window. I jerked my head up to see what was what, and I saw a dark shape hurtling my way, just slamming across the road, ignoring the cars and everything else.

It was Rattail, streaking at a fast waddle, right across JFK Drive, dodging cars, booking it. He was moving about as fast as I'd ever seen him go, even faster than the night of the flaming shopping cart.

"Da-*ark!*" He swarmed straight up the tree, ignoring all the people who'd stopped on the path and were gawking up at us. He was seriously out of breath. "The coyotes—over by the duck lake—

there's something—you won't believe this—I have to tell you—"

"I know—they mixed it up with Early, and he got his leg bitten. I was there."

"They're dead."

"What?" I felt my body stiffen up—muscles, insides, everything. "Rattail, what—?"

"The coyotes are dead, both of them."

I stared at him. He was panting, his nose wrinkled up, his teeth showing.

"Men came, in a truck. They had these weapons— guns or something, I guess—and the coyotes . . . the coyotes . . . they came out of their lair. And the men from the truck killed them. They pointed their guns and there was noise and smoke and the coyotes fell down and now they're dead. They got killed dead, right there in the middle of the park, in the sun and everything!"

I sat there in total silence, trying to absorb that. I don't think I blinked for a couple of minutes. The pictures that were trying to untangle themselves in my head, trying to make some sense somehow, weren't nice.

"Dark?"

He was wide-eyed, and his paws were twitching. Poor Rattail—he didn't like the coyotes any more than I did. But he was freaked and twitchy, and so was I. It took me a moment to figure out that the reaction came from having to look at the power the people had over us: over our lives, and our deaths.

They had power over everything in the park. No one likes to have their nose rubbed in the fact that someone can hurt you, kill you. No one wants to believe that you can't do a single thing to stop it. It makes you feel small, and pointless.

"Dark, did you hear me?"

I blinked, finally, and let my claws retract. I hadn't realized they'd come out. "I heard you. I'm just trying to think about this, understand it. The coyotes—those two coyotes over by Elk Glen Lake, anyway—men came with guns and shot them. But why did they shoot them? Because they bit Early?"

"Is that what those weapons are called, for sure? Guns?" He licked his lips. "Yes, they were all talking. They were talking to some people who were there when it happened, when that woman let Early run loose and the coyotes attacked him—"

"They didn't attack him."

What was I doing, defending them? I ought to be celebrating, sleeping a little easier; that was two coyotes I didn't have to worry about anymore. The park was now two coyotes safer, for all of us. So why was I feeling scared and angry and outraged?

"Early started it, Rattail. I was there. I saw. He knew where their lair was, and he went over to find them and throw down the challenge. I'm pretty sure he got bit because he got too close to—"

I stopped. Something, a picture, was moving around, fuzzy and unclear and half-remembered at the back of my eyes. . . .

"Dark?"

That was it. A dream I'd had, dozing fitfully in the tree, sharing the nightspace, the dreamspace, with Casablanca. Bastet, yes, there had been dreams of Bastet in the waning hours of the night, but I remembered now that there had also been dreams of a pair of coyotes who had babies to protect, coyotes whose eyes didn't look like dirty frost on a chilly predawn patch of desolation. I remembered the world of dream; there had been Sal's voice in my head, and coyotes. And Casablanca had dreamed the same.

"Dark, what's the matter?"

I stared straight into Rattail's face. I could taste something bitter at the back of my throat. I could name it, too. It was outrage. I could hear it sliding into my voice, making it a growl and a warning.

"It isn't fair."

"What's not fair?"

"Rattail, listen." I don't know why it felt so important to make him understand, but it did. "This is wrong. It's wrong and not right and not fair. Early getting bitten? That was his own fault. I was there. I saw!"

"How could it be his fault?" He was trying to understand why I was reacting the way I was. "No one made them bite him. They didn't have to."

"Yes, they did. You know how you told me Prairie gets when she has baby raccoons to take care of? How she gets fierce and nuts and she charges anything that comes too close? The coyotes were protecting babies, Rattail. Early told me that himself, and then he went and got up in their faces. He said he was going to, because this was his turf and he wasn't letting some coyotes challenge him. He's just a big coward anyway—he talks tough, but the minute anyone calls him on it, he puts his tail between his legs and wails like a whipped puppy."

Rattail didn't look bewildered anymore. "He was the one who went and bothered them? Just because he could? What kind of stupid reason is that to pick a fight?"

"Don't ask me—I think it's pretty stupid, too. But he started it, Rattail. If he'd left them alone, they would have stayed in the lair with their babies. If the gun people were going to shoot anyone, it should have been him, not them. Or maybe they should have shot that stupid woman who can't be bothered putting Early on a leash. This was her fault, too, just as much as his. Maybe more, letting him run loose when she knows she isn't supposed to."

He was quiet now, watching me. He hadn't seen me like this before. I wasn't sure I'd ever been this way before. And out of nowhere, I'd started to shake, shivering all over.

"All they did was stand up for their babies." There was a hot, tight feeling in my chest and stomach, as if I wanted to bring up a hairball. "How could the people shoot them for doing that? Did they shoot the babies, too? Rattail, have you heard anything like that?"

"No. Nothing. I don't think the people knew there were babies." I guess maybe shivering must be contagious, because he started in doing it, too. "I saw—I saw it, Dark. I watched it happen, from the tree. The coyotes fell down, with blood on their heads. And the people who did that, they walked over and nudged them with their feet. I guess they were making sure the coyotes really were dead, that it was safe. And they picked the coyotes up, and they tossed them in the back of their truck, and they drove away. They just threw them in the back, all limp—like the coyotes were stuff you'd throw in a Dumpster."

I swallowed hard. There was something about that picture that upset me maybe worse than the shooting.

"Everyone was talking and yelling—the people, I mean. I saw Memorie up high, circling—I want to talk to her about this, see what she thinks we should do." Rattail shook himself all over, as if he'd got drenched with water no one else could see. "Dark, I'm confused. I mean, I'm happy two of the coyotes are gone, but if there are babies, won't they starve? That's not right. The people shouldn't just leave them to starve."

"Yeah, there be babies there."

My head whipped around. The voice came from just behind us, in the tree itself: singsong, a little distant, a little sad.

"There be babies there, for sure. They not be there too long, though. Need to fend for themselves now. Can't be hunting from a hole in the ground."

I'm just amazed I didn't fall out of the tree. I hadn't heard Sal come up, and pretty much every nerve tightened up hard when I heard her voice behind me.

And Rattail actually *did* fall out of the tree. It wasn't very far—just down to the next set of branches—and he wouldn't have got hurt anyway, because we weren't that far off the ground in the first place. It would have actually been funny, if I'd felt like laughing at all, about anything.

"I scare you, Dark-as-night? Sorry 'bout that." She looked even smaller than I remembered, her dark wrinkled face poking out from a bundle of moving rags. "Hey, looky-look, I see a raccoon. I'm guessing you found that friend you misplaced the other day?"

"Hi, Sal. I didn't see you climb the tree." I looked down, watching Rattail shake himself, give an outraged little chattery noise, and pull himself up the tree again. "Yes, that's Rattail. He was okay after all—he spent that night with my cat friend, Casablanca, indoors. Oh, that's right—she says she knows you. Rattail, are you okay? This is Sal. Sal, this is my friend Rattail."

"Pleased." She wasn't smiling; I think she knew how silly he felt, falling out of the tree like that, and she didn't want to offend his dignity. "Dark, here, she was worried about you yesterday. Told her it was likely okay—I know how hard it is for anyone or anything to put a serious hurt on a raccoon, except maybe another raccoon, but you know friends, they like that and they worry."

"Hi." He sounded perilously close to sulky. "Pleased, too."

All of a sudden, she stopped being Sal who was carefully not smiling to avoid offending a dignified raccoon, and became someone else. I watched as her face changed and did something else altogether. She looked distant, remote, sad, but in a faraway kind of way. It made her look as if nothing out there could touch her—not men with guns, not coyotes, not wind or rain or the passage of time. And her voice went there, too. The change came right out of nowhere.

"Them cowboys from the Department of Agriculture, with their guns—that's a bad thing right there, them doing that. Fact of them doing it ain't near as bad as the reason why. Might be a reason that had some sense to it, but wasn't any sense in the one they used."

"Why did they do it, Sal? Wasn't it because the coyotes bit Early? Or was it something else?"

"Well, now, you might say so. You might even get folks to believe it, if they wanted to bad enough. Except that ain't the reason, little Miss Dark. That's just a fancy, convenient lie they keep, to tell the newspapers, and maybe themselves. After all, they people, right? They got to listen to the voices in their head, telling them they done wrong."

Still sad, distant, as far away as the moon. Something about how she was sitting, or what she was saying, had made an impression on Rattail. He was listening with both ears and the rest of his body, too, his tail stiff. And Sal looked like part of the tree itself, her rag sleeves all stuffed with dried grass, shaking loose in little wisps and being carried away by the breeze.

"See, right about now, there's a lot of weeping and wailing and *oh how sad the poor coyotes* going on out there. There's gonna be people writing letters, saying how horrible, the poor coyotes. So those guys at the Department of Agriculture, they got to try to spin it, let everyone know they did it because the coyotes went and hurt a poor little dog. But that ain't why. That's just sassafras and boiled lies, and they know it, too."

"But then why—?"

"Babygirl, you need to clean the winter out your ears and think straight. Because you ain't doing that, not right now." She shook her head at me. "You got to look at it and see it for what it is. You want me to spell it out, I can do that. You listening to me?"

I waited. Rattail settled down. Sal's lips hardly seemed to be moving, but we could hear her perfectly.

"Lots of people out there come in this park, just to take care of the animals. Not all Blanks, either, is it?

You and your friends, you got your own people coming in every night. Only reason you miss a meal is maybe because you too slow to get there, and someone else beats you to the pile. Don't make no difference what the weather's doing, they come in here and they get wet, they get cold, but that don't matter to them, so long as you get fed. Ain't that right, now?"

I was beginning to see where she was going, just a little glimmer of light. "You know it is. Jack and Angie, you mean. So—?"

"That their names? Jack and Angie? Well, now, they been on the phone with Animal Control, coming up on months now. People been calling up the boss lady about them coyotes since before the summer ever showed up. People been calling and calling, like to burn the ears off those Control folk. They been taking calls and they didn't do diddly, not until today."

"You're saying the City people knew all about it?" Rattail sounded shocked. Funny thing, I'd never seen him shocked before, not even when he'd told me about his own father going crazy-bad Danger and hurting him.

I looked at Sal, huddled up in the tree, her rags pulled tight around her. The afternoon was getting chilly; it was going to be a cold night, and I suddenly had a picture in my head: the two baby coyotes, curled up tight to their mother, nursing and warm against the cold, curling up against each other for warmth instead, hungry, waiting for a meal that wasn't coming.

Sal tilted her head at me. "Well, what you think? Course they knew. They knew you all were in trouble. You tell me something, Dark: you ever seen anyone drive in and start shooting coyotes before today? You hear tell of any suchlike?"

I understood now. She'd said it: they'd done it for a bad reason. It was coming clear in my head. I opened my mouth to say something, to try and make it even clearer by sharing the words. But Sal wasn't done yet.

"Fifty people been calling Animal Control, maybe a hundred people, who knows how many. It's coming up on months the people been calling in, and no one did a thing about it, right? So how come a few people call in on their cell phones, yelling that coyotes come out and bit some woman's dog, and here comes men with guns?"

I had the words I wanted now. It was all the way clear, what she meant. "You're saying they don't care about protecting us. They don't care at all. That's not why they shot the coyotes. Is it?"

"I'm sorry, babycat." She'd seen me figure it out, and she knew it had to hurt. "But no, that ain't why. They weren't protecting the dog that got bit because he's a dog. They were protecting that dog—what you say his name is, Early?—because that dog be someone's property."

"But . . ."

Rattail's voice died away. I saw the light go off for him as he caught up with both of us.

He tried again. "I don't want that to be right. It can't be right. Because what you mean is, they're abandoning us to the coyotes. They won't protect us because they think we're homeless. We're supposed to belong to someone, and we don't. That if we don't belong to someone, we don't have any value. They don't care if we die. And that can't be right!"

His voice had gone all the way up, a high angry

squeak. Maybe it wasn't anger—it might have been despair. Despair was what I was feeling, for sure.

"No, it ain't right." Sal's voice was soft, quiet, resigned. "But it's true."

CHAPTER TWELVE

I think it was right after the two coyotes got shot that things started to feel different in the park. Or maybe it was right after that conversation with Sal—I'm not sure. I just know that the way I felt about everything to do with the park seemed to change, and not in a good way.

One thing was for sure: it changed the way Rattail thought and felt. And that was the first thing I had to deal with.

It's not like I was thinking about it—not with my head, anyway. It was really more about feeling than thinking. Thinking about stuff isn't usually the smartest way to stay healthy out here, anyway. You listen to your insides first, all those instincts—*Uh-oh, there's*

182

something chasing you, better move, go, fast, straight up and don't look down until you can't hear it breathing behind you anymore, and hope that whatever it is, it can't climb trees—that's when thinking gets useful, when you can listen to things work out inside your head.

We watched Sal climb back down the tree. We had our heads together, but we weren't saying anything yet. There was something about the way she moved that didn't really look like climbing; I couldn't figure out the mechanics of how she got back to the ground, and I was watching her all the way. It was very strange— there was this tiny little person, wearing old rags and leaves, with all those funky dried plants she'd picked up around the park falling out of her sleeves every time she moved. I noticed that her shoes didn't match and that they seemed much too big to even stay on her feet, much less let her go climbing trees like a cat. She had her feet wrapped up inside the shoes, though, lots more rags and dried grass and things, so maybe that made it easier for her to get around. However she was doing it, she got down the tree and disappeared off into the bushes almost as neatly as I could do it.

"Do you believe what she said?"

I jerked my head. There was something in Rattail's voice I hadn't heard there before, something moving around, a feeling that was twisting and turning, just out of reach. I couldn't figure out just what it was. All I knew was that I didn't like it. He suddenly didn't sound like himself anymore.

"About them not caring unless people own us? Yes. At least, I think I do. But it was just her opinion, Rattail. Unless—do you mean believing her, like, was she telling us a lie? Why would Sal lie?"

Now that I was thinking about it, the idea left a bad taste at the back of my throat. What was the point of trusting anyone, if all you could ever be was someone's property? And even if you were willing to be their property, what was to stop them from getting rid of you, losing you, selling you, dumping you . . . ?

"How should I know? How should I know why people do anything? I think maybe they're all crazy-bad, under the skin."

It was still there in his voice, that hard little curly thing, and out of nowhere, I suddenly got what it was: bitterness.

"Rattail, no! That's not fair." A voice in my head was asking, *Why am I arguing with him?* Rattail was my best friend and I loved him, but I hated what he was saying—hated it enough so that I couldn't just ignore it. "Sal's not crazy-bad. Neither are Jack and Angie. It's like Sal said, they come here every night and they get cold and wet and tired and they don't care; they come here and make sure we don't go hungry. How can you call that crazy, or bad? And Jesse's not crazy-bad, either. So maybe he knows a crazy-bad—that guy Billy is a Danger, for sure—but Jesse's a Warm."

He was quiet for a moment. Down below, a woman was putting something up on a lamppost, some kind of poster. She had a stack of them, a pile big enough for me to see from up the tree. She made sure it was up, that the wind wouldn't blow it away, and then moved up along the street, putting up the papers as she went. There was writing, big letters and small, and some kind of photograph—a cat or a dog—I couldn't quite see.

"I don't trust them." If Rattail had noticed the woman or her papers, he wasn't saying so. "Give me one good reason to trust them."

It was the way he said it that made me understand. Just a simple sentence, but he was ice-cold, not
moving, no warmth in it anywhere. I felt a kind of
prickling across my skin, and I felt my muscles want
to tense up.

I got it now, that voice in my head again: *Everything is going to be different.* There are no words for
how much I hate that.

I tried again. "Rattail, listen. If you think Jack and
Angie are crazy-bads, you're wrong. You've been eating all the food they put out for you, haven't you? And
Sam, the man Jasper lives with, what about him? He
went and talked to the police, tried to make them
understand about the coyotes. He didn't have to do
that—"

He was hunched up, his shoulders as hard and
tight as his voice was. "I don't care. I don't trust any
of them, not anymore. Why should I? Why do you?
Trusting them is stupid. If Sal was right, they all
think it's okay for us to just die unless they can own
us. How can you trust anyone who thinks like that?"

I gawked at him. It was just so different, and so
hard to believe. This was the same raccoon who came

out, night after night, and put on a show for Jack and Angie. He flirted with them, did little dances, acted like some kind of street performer, sitting up on his haunches, making them laugh. He worked for his supper. I'd always thought he liked doing that.

"Give me a reason, Dark. Just one reason."

He was watching me, and it occurred to me that he wasn't just talking; he was waiting for an answer. And I didn't know what I wanted to say. He was wrong about the main thing, but he was right, too. At least, I could see why he'd feel the way he did.

But I had to say something, because this was Ratty, and he'd asked me a question and I owed him an answer. I opened my mouth, but I didn't know what was going to come out.

"One reason? Okay. I don't think they're all the same. That's why. And Sal didn't say she thought all the people thought we only matter if they could own us. She wasn't talking about everyone. She was just talking about some people."

"I don't care. How do I know she's right, or even telling the truth? You had people, and as soon as they had a baby, they threw you away like you were just leftovers from their supper. What about Casablanca? They just went away and left her. Seems to me people do that kind of thing all the time. So you give me one good reason to think any of them really care about what happens to us. Give me one good reason to think they care about anything but being on top. Come on, Dark. Just one reason. I'm still waiting."

I didn't answer right away, because I couldn't. What he'd said, about being about as important as leftovers? That hurt. I don't know whether he knew it, or whether he meant it to hurt when he said it. Maybe he was hoping it would change my mind about things. But I couldn't worry about that right then. There were other more important, more immediate things.

"Okay. So maybe we do need to be careful, more careful. Maybe we need to look out for each other even more than we used to. But that's the coyote's fault, Rattail. Why should I blame the people? Why should you? They didn't bring the coyotes, the coyotes just came."

He was quiet, still hunched and cautious. Something was coming clear in my head. I trusted Jesse and Sal. I'd trusted them with my feelings right away.

Sal had spoken into my heart and my memory, taken me into a safe place where I was adored and protected, the goddess of cats, people chanting my name. And Jesse had stood there with me in his arms, with a big dog who could have ripped me apart at his feet and the two coyotes just a few yards away, and I'd known, through my skin and down into every part of me, that there could have been twenty dogs sitting at Jesse's feet and a hundred coyotes lined up with their teeth bared, and he wouldn't have let them come near me or hurt me.

I hadn't stopped to think about why I'd trusted him; I just had, because my instinct told me that was the smart thing to do. If I thought the way Rattail was thinking, it would mean not trusting my instincts. And if I couldn't do that, I was dead, because what else could I trust?

And Ratty wasn't going to understand. I could tell.

"Listen, Rattail, please? It doesn't matter if we agree about trusting the people. But we have to trust each other—that does matter. I wish I could believe the people were going to take the coyotes away from here. I don't know which people, the people from the Control place, maybe. But I don't believe it. And okay, I do trust the Warms and Sal and Jesse. I just knew right away that I could trust them, and I have to believe what I knew. Don't you get it? If I can't trust my own feelings, then I have nothing at all, and I won't last a minute out here. And if you don't know that, you should by now."

He licked his lips. He was still listening. I didn't know if he was actually hearing what I was saying, though. It occurred to me that I didn't have to make him agree with me. All I had to do was make him understand.

Down below, the paper on the lamppost was waving a little bit in the breeze, the corners sort of flapping. People were walking, talking, driving by; a few of them stopped long enough to look at the poster, shake their heads, and keep on walking. A chilly little wind had come up, lifting my fur, moving across my back as if I were covered in grass. I turned back to Rattail.

"I'll tell you this much. Just because I trust them, that doesn't mean I'm going to depend on them to protect us. Because we can't. And that means we have to protect each other."

I licked him, washing his shoulder, his chin, the side of his face. I felt him relax—not all the way, but some.

"I'll watch your back." The shoulder was nice and damp and clean; I moved up and began on his ears, and felt the tension in his muscles lighten up a bit more. Good. "I promise, Rattail. Whenever we're together, I'll watch your back. If something's coming, I'll let you know. And that goes for Casablanca, too. This is all about us, you and me and Casablanca and Memorie, all taking care of each other. Okay?"

He sighed, and I suddenly got why he'd been so tight: he'd been holding his breath. No wonder he'd looked all bunched up. "Okay. Dark, what do you think we ought to do about those baby coyotes? I don't want to go near them, but I don't think it's okay to just let them starve to death, either. Should we tell Memorie? Maybe she can think of something to do about it."

I put one paw on his head and began washing the top of his head, right between his ears. Funny fur, soft and bristly at the same time.

"Of course we have to tell Memorie. But what do you want to bet she already knows? Memorie knows everything that happens in the park, pretty much. Doesn't she?"

"Well, sure. And if she knows, maybe she can come up with some ideas. I think we need someone smart to tell us what to do about it."

He'd loosened up, and that was good. It made things seem more like normal. They weren't, though, and I didn't think they ever would be again. I couldn't fool myself into thinking we'd ever get back to where we were before the coyotes came, before the Control people had come into the park with guns. Realizing that left me feeling sad, and a little sick.

We stayed where we were until nightfall, dozing and watching. I napped in little fits and spurts, never really relaxing my mind all the way. There was one thing I didn't know about coyotes, and I was hoping Memorie could tell me. The question was going to bother me until I found out the answer.

We got lucky with timing that day. Rattail and I came to a sort of unspoken agreement—we both thought we needed to talk to Memorie before Jack and Angie showed up with our food. But we needed to talk to Casablanca, too. If she'd been out of the park all day, there was a chance she hadn't heard what happened, and that was no good. We couldn't watch out for each other unless we all knew what was going on.

Normally, Casablanca stayed hidden until well after sunset. That day, though, the crowds in the park seemed to thin out a lot earlier than usual. Maybe it was the whole mess with the shooting, or maybe they just felt the winter coming in. Whatever it was, Ratty and I both noticed it.

We were just getting ready to climb down when something rustled down below, and there was Casablanca's cream-colored pointy face, peering at us through the leaves.

She nodded at me and rubbed her cheek against Rattail. Casablanca's big on scent-marking things. "Hey. You hear about those two coyotes getting killed?"

"Oh, good, you already know." That was a big relief, and a big time-saver, too. "Casablanca, there are babies. The stupid people with the guns didn't bother going in and rescuing the pups—they just left them there, alone. I don't think they're going to survive unless someone does something for them. We were going to talk to Memorie about it."

She'd moved on to washing her feet, but she paused and thought about it. "Good call. Shame about the babies. Hate the coyotes, but this isn't fair. Can't let them starve. Someone needs to handle it. Not me, though."

Getting that conversation with Memorie was going to be tricky, since it had to happen between our food and her hunting. But that night, of all nights, Jack and Angie showed up a couple of hours early. I don't know who was more surprised: us to see them just when we wanted them, or them to find all three of us sitting there, waiting for them to show. I noticed that Rattail wasn't doing his usual flirty routine with them. That gave me a little ache under my ribs. Like I said, I don't like it when things change.

"Hey, kitties. Hey, silly coon." Angie was opening cans and pouring out piles of dry food. "Jack, I think there's something wrong with Rattail—he's really quiet tonight. Um . . . could I get a little help here? What are you looking at?"

"Someone lost their dog."

Jack was looking at the poster, and I looked up from my pile and finally got a good look at it. I couldn't read the words, but there were big black letters on top, smaller ones down below, and right in the middle there was a photograph of a yellow dog.

"Oh, man, Angie, this is terrible. She's a rescue dog, a yellow lab mix—she was being fostered and she broke away in the park and no one's seen her since. That was the day before yesterday, near the playground. It says her name is Iris."

Angie set the big plastic tub of dry food down a few feet away from us and went over to stand next to Jack. I saw something happen to her face—for just a moment, she looked like the woman when they'd dumped me and she hadn't been sure about it, her mouth puckering and her eyes crinkling up like a baby trying not to cry. "This is so sad. 'Iris was badly abused as a puppy. She's very shy and timid, and may be frightened of people, so please, if you see her, call the number below, instead of trying to approach her.' God, I hate people sometimes. There are days I'm ashamed to be a member of this species. How badly do we suck?"

Rattail had gone through his pile faster than usual, and he was obviously still hungry. I saw him throw a cautious look at Jack and Angie, making sure they were staying where they were for the moment, looking at the poster and not him. Then he came down off the hillside where they always put his food, sat up on his haunches, and got the top of the dry-food tub off. He dipped his paw in and came out with one mouthful, two, three . . .

"I think we should take a drive around when we're done with the kitties. Call for the dog, see if we can get her to come out." Jack turned around to look at Angie and caught Rattail in the act, shoveling food into his mouth straight from the big plastic tub. "Hey! Back up, raccoon! You want more food, I'll give you some, but learn some manners!"

Rattail skittered back up the hill, out of reach, watching them. Jack was shaking his head, and Angie was smiling; Jack popped the lid back on the food tub, but he poured Ratty another small pile first. It all looked normal, but it wasn't. Rattail wasn't playing or showing off—he was watchful, cautious, distant. And the Warms, who liked him, would never know that.

Maybe because it was so early, Jack and Angie didn't feel any need to make sure we got to eat uninterrupted; after all, the coyotes usually didn't come out until after sunset. Or maybe they were just anxious, worrying about that missing dog, Iris. Whatever their reasons were, they left while we were still eating. That was another piece of good timing, because it left us free to go find Memorie. It was weird, but I kept thinking that the coyote pups hadn't had food since the morning. That couldn't be good. Babies need to eat a lot, and often.

And of course, just as we were getting ready to slip off and head over to Memorie's tree, she came to us.

I heard the rustle from above, the rush of air as she let her wings glide her to a perch up high, and then her voice, high and passionless and sort of comforting, somehow, calling us from the treetop. I had a sudden feeling—a certainty, really: no matter what else might change in the park, life and death and love or anything else, Memorie's voice would always sound just this way.

We went up the tree, all three of us. Memorie was there, wings folded and tucked, talons holding on to the branch, that oval face of hers still impossible to read. She rustled a bit, reseating herself.

"You were coming to me. I heard you as I circled. Easier, much easier, for one to fly than for three to walk."

"True. Thanks." Casablanca shot me a sideways look. It was a clear signal: *You were there, you talk.* I turned to Memorie.

"It's about the coyotes." Memorie would know, I thought. She seemed to know pretty much everything. "About the pups."

"Ah. The little ones, left behind. Yes. You want to know how old they must be before they can survive on their own?"

"Yes. No. Well, partly." So she didn't know everything after all. "I want to know how old they have to be before they start hunting. Not exactly the same thing."

"A question hard to answer." The oval turned my way, and I saw her blink. "There are two of them, babes of a yearling female. They are small, not new but not yet ready to hunt. They will need care, if the choice to preserve them is made."

"Don't want to." Casablanca was hunched up. "They grow up, more of them hunting us. Besides—don't want one of them to eat me. Maybe not old enough to do that now. But they will be."

"And the people won't help us." Rattail sounded bitter. "They don't care what happens to us. But they killed the coyotes and now someone has to feed the pups. I don't understand what you mean, about choosing to preserve them. What else could we do?"

"We could let them starve."

I heard myself say it and shook my head. The others were watching me. "After all, 'Blanca's right. Why do we want two more coyotes rampaging through the park? So we could let them die, except we won't. Will we?"

"No." Casablanca—if I was hearing her right—was totally disgusted. I wasn't sure what she was disgusted about: having to save a couple of coyote pups, or the suggestion that we could let them starve. "So now what? What do we do?"

Memorie lifted her shoulders, and I saw the great wings begin to lift. "For this moment, nothing at all. Leave this with me. But if you—any of you, all of you—will come to Elk Glen Lake, you will see what I have done. Good night to you, and good hunting. Stay safe."

CHAPTER THIRTEEN

One day, two days. The sun kept rising and setting, just as if nothing were different. There was no news, no word about the coyote pups.

Everything was the same. Everything was different.

Jack and Angie came to feed us at night, the way they always did. We ate, just as usual. I was listening to them as I ate, listening hard, paying closer attention. After all, the reality was that the people were the ones with the power, not us. So it made sense to me, knowing who was with me, who was against me, knowing what they were all doing. It was just like anything else out here: the more you know, the better your chances are of staying alive.

During the day, I mostly stayed in my favorite tree. Rattail hung out with me, just as usual. We were a little more watchful than we had been, after the sun went down; we were a little more careful during those hours when the sun was rising or setting, too, because that was the coyotes' time to hunt. After all, the two coyotes who were gone weren't the only ones in the park.

The mist had become something new and unwelcome. Two nights running, it came at us from both directions, curling up from the wet cold grass and settling from the treetops as the cloud cover blew in from the water. And it wasn't just a place I could hide in, not anymore. I suddenly understood that it was a place where anything could hide. I knew—in my head, anyway—that the mist had always been just that. But it felt, I don't know, scarier, more ominous, less safe.

At night, Jack and Angie seemed more watchful, looking around them, staying with us longer, making sure we'd finished and headed for safe places before they moved on to whoever they were feeding next. They were still worried about that missing dog,

Iris—when they did drive away after we'd eaten, they drove even more slowly than usual, and I could hear both of them, calling for the dog: *Iris, here Iris, it's okay sweetie, Iris . . .* Their voices would get fainter and fainter as they drove away toward the west, the car becoming nothing more than two tiny points of dull red, swallowed by the mist.

I pointed that out to Rattail. I tried to make him see that mistrusting everyone, even the people who were obviously on his side, was stupid—it was depriving him of something that could mean safety. But that was another change, another different thing: I couldn't get through to Rattail at all. He was there with me as much as he'd ever been, at least he seemed to be. His reactions had even sharpened, when he thought anything could be a threat.

He also talked to me less. And not all of him was there—some part of him that had been open before had closed up, since that conversation in the tree with Sal.

The conversations Jack and Angie were having with each other were a little different, too. Ever since I'd first shown up there, they'd chattered just as much about how cool we were as they did about anything else, except when they'd talked to Sam about people stuff. But Sam hadn't been around in a little while, and Jack and Angie were saying less, and when they did, it was short, to the point, and mostly about real things: the coyotes, the missing dog. Some of what they started talking about had nothing to do with us or the park at all—it was about presidents and war and politics and stuff like that.

Casablanca—okay, so she wasn't different, so far as I could see. But I could have been wrong about that. Casablanca was pretty hard to read. She'd have to suddenly start barking like a dog or something for a change to really be noticeable.

Two days, three days, nothing at all. There was no word back from Memorie—there'd been no sign of her shadow overhead, no rush of those long wings to tell me she was nearby. So there was no news, and if Rattail had hooked up with her without me, he wasn't letting me know.

I didn't like that idea, that my best friend was maybe keeping secrets from me. It hurt. But there wasn't anything I could do about it, and I didn't want to make things even worse by asking about it. So I kept quiet, not liking the way things felt, and waited.

Two days, three days. On the third day, I was dozing up in my tree, when I heard my name called from just down below.

"Dark? You there?"

I opened my eyes, wide awake nice and fast. I was alone—Rattail had been there when I closed my eyes, but he'd gone down while I slept, and so had the sun. It was just about full twilight, and the park was a lot quieter than it had been. "Jesse? Is that you? Should I come down?"

"If you would. If not, I can come back later. I don't want to mess with your dinner schedule."

"Now's good. It's going to be a while before food gets here. Give me a second, okay?"

I stretched, letting the muscles in my back and legs ripple and flex, arching my spine, sharpening my claws. That taken care of, I went down the tree, headfirst as usual. "Wow, it got cold out here!"

It really was cold, the bad kind you feel in your joints. We'd had some rainy nights and a couple of rainy days, but those weren't actually cold, not unless the wind had come up—nights when the park was both wet and windy, now *that* was hard-chilly. But this was a different kind of cold; it was clear out there today, clear enough so that I'd known the cold was coming, a hard sharp sky in a shade of blue that looked like faraway water waiting to freeze, like a sheet of blue ice hanging over my head. Sitting on the paved path at Jesse's feet, I could feel the temperature drop as a series of tiny chilly shocks, traveling up through the pads of my paws, settling into my shoulders like a warning: *Buckle up, cat, winter's here, get that winter coat growing, there are cold dark nights ahead.*

"I was going to head over toward Elk Glen Lake." Jesse had a different jacket on than the one he'd on before. This one had fleecy fur sticking out around the top and cuffs. It looked like the same stuff my cat bed had been made from, back when I had one of those. "I've been out of the park since yesterday, and I kind of want to know what's been going on. Would you like to come along? And do you want a ride?"

I did it again, just jumped straight from the ground into his arms—no thinking; no worrying, nothing.

That settled it for me, right there: I was right and Rattail was wrong. I trusted my instincts and I was going to keep on doing just that.

Jesse grinned down at me. "Whoa, I guess you do want a ride. Hi."

I wasn't cold anymore; he'd unzipped the jacket and let me snuggle down inside. I'd been right about it being the same woolly fleecy stuff my bed had been lined with, and it was familiar in a good-hurt kind of way. I knew how my claws would catch in those particular loops, how it would feel against my cheek and the base of my ear, how my whiskers would fold against it when I'd rested in one place too long. "Is this a new jacket? Is that why you went out of the park, to get a new jacket?"

"No. No, I went to see my mother. The jacket was in my closet, over at her house—in my old room. It was a birthday present from her, a long time ago. I've never worn it before—I actually forgot all about it, but she reminded me. She gets worried that I'll catch cold and die or something."

His voice was sad, in a way I couldn't really identify. Not crying-sad, more like distant, faraway-sad, the kind of sad you get with an old pain you know you can't do anything about.

"It's nice and warm." I was relaxing for the first time since the coyotes, but there was something back there in my head, and I remembered how he'd sounded, talking to his crazy friend Billy. There had been a very different tone in his voice when he said the word *father* than there was about his mother.

It wasn't my business, though, and I wasn't going to ask. If he wanted to tell me, he could; it was his choice. But there was one thing I wanted to ask him about.

"Jesse, how come you can talk to me? And to the dogs? Did you have to learn to do that, or could you always?"

If he minded me asking, that didn't show. "No clue. I was always sort of able to do it, with Sugaree—that was my cat at home, when I was kid. I don't have any brothers or sisters, and talking to my parents wasn't any good. So I started talking to Sugaree, and I guess maybe she wanted someone to talk to. After a while, it just kind of happened. And then when I moved mostly into the park, I started talking to Nightmare when Billy wasn't listening, and it turned out I could understand the dog, too, and he could understand me." He changed the subject. "Still liking the jacket?"

"Yep. I used to have a bed made out of this stuff. All fleecy."

He bent his head and looked down at me. My own head was the only part of me that wasn't zipped in; I wouldn't have minded having my ears be warm, too, but there was something about trying to talk to him through a coat that just felt rude.

"So did Sugaree," he told me. "That cat bed was her favorite place in the world. When she got really old, that's how we knew she was getting ready to die, before she even told me she was going to Bubastis: she stopped sleeping in her bed and wanted to sleep on my bed instead."

"Did you let her?" I was sniffing the inside of the jacket and thinking he'd been telling the truth about it being so new. The only strong scent anywhere was fabric, and some thread; I could just pick up the very faint beginnings of Jesse-scent.

"Of course I did. Sugaree was my best friend."

He reached down and tickled the spot right between my ears. That was one of my favorite things, and I heard myself start to purr.

"Oh, cool! You have the same skritch-nerve-link thing on your head that Sugaree had. I miss having a cat around. Hey, are you hungry? I was going to head out of the park a little later, maybe get a burrito on Haight Street—I didn't want to stay and have anything at my mom's place, so I haven't eaten anything yet today. We could stop at the market and get some cat food for you. You up for that?"

"Okay. Sounds good."

I heard myself say it, the words just popping out, and out of nowhere, I started wondering just what part of my instincts had suddenly turned off, or on, or both. Because even though I trusted Jesse, that suggestion still should have made me think before I answered.

I hadn't been out of the park since the Dumping, even though Casablanca had told me it was cool for me to come hang out with her when the weather got bad. The park—mist and raccoons and gophers and friends and coyotes and everything else about it—was my home now, the only one I had. The idea of leaving it should have scared me half to death.

But it didn't. Riding along with Jesse, that sounded okay. And even if I got back too late for dinner with Rattail and Casablanca, Jesse would feed me.

"It's okay—we don't have to if you don't feel comfortable about it. I just thought you might want an early dinner." We'd turned down past where I'd first met Rattail, heading toward the ocean, and toward Elk Glen Lake. I wasn't sure how he'd known I was thinking about it—maybe I'd stiffened up.

"I do. Thank you."

We kept going. If I was getting heavy, Jesse wasn't showing it; he had one arm cupped under me, outside the jacket, and he didn't seem to be feeling tired. Neither of us said anything, but the silence wasn't awkward—we just didn't feel any need to talk. I closed my eyes, synching up to the rhythm of his walk.

"Uh-oh. Swell. Heads-up, Dark—or down, I mean. Here comes a major pain in the butt."

There was something in his voice—disgust, maybe some amusement, or resignation. He stopped walking.

My eyes popped open. There was a car pulled over along the side of the road: a police cruiser. There were two cops in it, and one was getting out. I ducked down deep, and Jesse zipped the jacket up nearly to the top.

"Well, hey there." The words were friendly, but the tone of voice wasn't friendly at all: it was smug and just a little mean, and it kind of reminded me of Billy the Crazy-Bad. "Out for a nice little evening stroll, son? I've seen you out here before, haven't I? Matter of fact, I'm pretty sure I've chased you out of here before. You had a friend with you last time, didn't you? Big nasty boy with a big nasty dog? Yeah, I thought so. Care to show me a little ID?"

"Sure. Here you go, Officer." Jesse didn't sound worried, more like bored.

Quiet, while we stood and waited. I could hear the cop breathing through his nostrils. I thought he was going to come back at Jesse with that same snarky voice, but I was in for a surprise. When he finally spoke up, he sounded very different.

"Jesse Brangolder-Wyse. *Brangolder-Wyse.*" Maybe I was hungrier than I'd realized, because I seemed to be hallucinating—he sounded respectful. "Would that be—?"

Jesse didn't sound particularly respectful when he answered. There it was again, whatever I'd heard when he said "My father's a lawyer" to Billy, that night I'd been caught in the Dumpster and the coyote mother had slaughtered the Bunker Bunny as a hunting lesson for her pups. "Yes, Officer. It would. Yes, Robert Brangolder-Wyse is my father. Yes, I'm his son. Is this enough ID for you, Officer? Or do you need more? It's all I have on me, but I could always take a DNA test or something. I'm sure my father could get the results greenlighted for you at one of the city's labs, if you grovel hard enough when you ask him. Want to borrow some kneepads?"

Safe in the jacket, hidden away and curled against the front of Jesse's shirt, I flinched. There was no mistaking the edge on his voice—it was bitter and dark and had contempt in it. I couldn't figure out what was causing it, though: his father or the cop. I wondered if the cop was going to arrest him or hit him or something. No one likes to be talked to that way, and after all, the cop had all the power right now, not Jesse. But when the cop spoke again, his voice had smoothed out, all the way flat.

"Sorry to bother you, sir. Have a nice night."

I heard the car door slam and the sound of tires

as the police cruiser pulled away, hard and fast. For about a minute, we just stood there on the park path under the streetlamp, not going anywhere.

I stuck my head back out of the jacket and stared around. It was pretty dark now, but there were a couple, a man and woman, walking past and talking in soft voices. They saw my head sticking out of Jesse's jacket, did a double-take, and smiled. There was no sign of the police cruiser.

"Jesse?" I stared up at him. "I don't want to stick my nose in your business, but—well—what was that?"

We were walking again, turning down a curve in the road, and I recognized where we were, at the edge of the water-meadow leading out to the lake, where the coyote lair was. "You mean that stuff with the cop? People call that brownnosing. Or butt-kissing. Or sucking up."

I was quiet, just waiting. He sighed, his chest rippling, and me rippling along with it. There was no wind at all; he was looking around the lakeshore, and everything was dead calm.

"It's because of my father. My father is the city attorney. He's the Biggest Baddest Lawyer in Town.

So of course they're all scared to death of him—he can fire any of them. He'd do it, too—he's done it before. My father likes getting his name in the papers. And he takes his power very, very seriously."

"I'm sorry. I'm really sorry."

I wasn't sure what I was apologizing for, because I hadn't done anything, but his voice made me have to say something. Hate, the real thing—that's very scary when you hear it. It's very humbling, too. The way Jesse sounded reminded me of what happens to old tree branches when it rains too much—water gets inside, and they start splintering and rotting away. Everything gets damaged.

He shrugged, shoulders up and down, me up and down with him. "Not your fault, kitty. His fault. Mine, too, maybe. I only go home when I know he isn't going to be there—like I said, my mother gets worried. She knows I spend most of my time in the park. She's sure I'm going to get mugged or shot or eaten by bears or something. Mothers are like that, I guess. Doesn't help that I'm an only child."

"So why *do* you live in the park? You don't have to, right?"

What was it about this whole situation that was making me forget my manners? Now that I'd asked one thing, I wanted to know everything. The People used to say "Curiosity killed the cat," whenever I'd start nosing around something they didn't think I should have. They'd say it with affection, like they thought whatever I was doing was cute, but it was obviously something that other people say a lot. It's probably true, too, and mostly I just shut up and find out what I want to know without asking or annoying anyone. But Jesse made me want to know more, and besides, he didn't seem to mind telling me.

He looked down at me, and I could see the amusement on his face, nice and clear. "To make my father bleed inside, of course. He's spent his whole life making other people bleed inside—that's what Attorney Brangolder-Wyse does for fun and profit. He's as mean as a snake, and he gets away with being mean because he has power. I wouldn't care, except that the person he hurts the most is my mother. I can't do much about that, but he tried it on me, too. And I choose not to let him. There's this idea a lot of people have that you're supposed to let your parents get away with stuff just because they're your parents. That you have to respect them because they made you."

"You don't think so." It wasn't a question.

"Nope. If you want my respect, you have to earn it. My father? Not so much. He's a mean jerk. I may have to let him get away with it, but that doesn't mean I have to make it easy for him. Since I'm over eighteen, he can't make me do much of anything, and that includes living in his house and putting up with his garbage."

I was quiet, absorbing, thinking. My ears were busy filtering out the distant sounds of the world outside the park, listening for anything close by. And I was sniffing hard.

"Besides," he added, "I like it here. I like animals better than people, mostly. They're better conversationalists. What is it, Dark?"

"Hang on. . . ."

I was scenting something—a whiff of dog, different scents, more than one and too close by for comfort. Of course, I was safe where I was, but that didn't mean I wanted the coyotes to know I was here.

"We've got coyotes, Jesse. Pretty close to us—the smell's strong."

"I know—even I'm smelling it, and I'm no cat." He turned toward the lair, letting me pinpoint the location with eye and nose. "It's the babies. Are they out? I can't see that far."

"Not just the babies." I had it now: two sets of smells, not one. "They've got company."

Jesse glanced down at me. I had my head out of the jacket, straining off into the darkness. My eyes had picked up what Jesse's eyes couldn't, not without a flashlight or a big bright moon: a flash of yellow, soft-looking ears that flopped in a way that would never happen on a straight-eared coyote, and an anxious, short-muzzled face, looking out and around.

She came out of the lair first, leading the two pups. She was thin, too thin, as if she hadn't been eating enough since she'd broken the leash of the person who was trying to help her, and run off into the park. The two pups, right behind her, looked healthy and well fed.

Memorie had said to do nothing and leave it to her, that if we came to Elk Glen, we would see what she had done. This was what she'd meant: bringing the homeless yellow dog and the motherless pups together. I wondered whether the dog had any milk in her, any way to nurse the pups that weren't hers, any way to feed them unless she hunted. . . .

A movement above my head, and I jerked in Jesse's hold, the two of us turning our gaze upward. I heard a disturbance in the air, motion, something falling.

Thump.

Not more than a foot from Iris's muzzle, something hit the soft ground. I'd made out the shape as it fell: a very large possum. Dinner for either Iris or the pups.

We watched the owl circle; a huge sweeping arc of wing and straight back. Her talons, empty now, were out and ready—she wasn't done hunting yet. Maybe the next thing she caught would be for her, maybe more for Iris and her adopted litter. Either way, there would be more to come.

Memorie had said it herself more than once: everything in the park deserved a chance to earn its place. The sin the coyotes had committed was to take away chances. But as much danger as they meant to me and mine, the pups deserved their own chance.

"Well." Jesse turned his back on Iris, the young coyotes, the lair. "You ready to roll, Dark? Don't know about you, but I'm seriously ready for some dinner. Let's head over to Haight Street."

CHAPTER FOURTEEN

Three nights, four nights, five nights.

The rhythm of the park is like a drumbeat, one you hardly even notice because you're so used to it and it's so regular. Or maybe I mean a heartbeat: steady and even, never turning off. Stuff coming in from the outside world can affect it, make it jump high and hard or slow down, but only for a few hours. Mostly it just keeps on doing what it does. If it changes enough to make you notice, something's wrong somewhere.

Five nights, and life in the park kept on doing just what it had been doing since the night I was dumped there: moving along with its own rhythms.

Rattail was there, still quieter than he had been, but there, hanging out. He didn't seem to want to talk about the big stuff—the important stuff—at all. I thought about pushing it—after all, the coyotes weren't going away, and if the people who were supposed to be doing something about them weren't going to bother, then just sitting there and waiting for everything to blow up around us seemed pretty dumb to me. But when I tried to talk about it, he shut me down.

We were up our tree, two days after Jesse and I saw what Memorie had set up. I was a little freaked about Ratty, who'd shown up at dinner the night before with a nasty wound on his rear left leg. I'd seen that before, usually when one of the male raccoons mixed it up with another one. It happens mostly when they fight over food or maybe over a girl raccoon, and since Rattail didn't have to fight for food, I figured it was probably over his girlfriend Prairie, some other male trying to muscle his way in next to her.

He made it pretty clear that questions about it wouldn't be welcome. So I didn't ask, and he wasn't offering me information. Wherever he got that wound from, though, he was perfectly willing to let me to wash it for him, and of course I did, cleaning it and then washing the rest of him.

It was a funny thing—while I was washing him, and he was relaxing, a little voice popped into my head: *Something about that dog taking care of the pups really made you want a kitten to wash.* Which was a stupid thing to think, because no, I didn't. It was more of an instinct, me playing mother to Rattail when I groomed him. I'd been doing it since long before Iris took over for the dead coyote parents. Besides, he liked me doing it.

"Are you okay? This is pretty nasty." It was, too. The bite, if that's what it was, had left him missing too much fur, and the skin was puffy and oozing and didn't smell right.

He stuck his leg out and glared at it over his shoulder. "I think so. Hurts, but I'd be more worried if it didn't."

That made me feel better, because it sounded a lot more normal for him. "What does the other raccoon look like? He must have been a real coward, biting you from behind. I hope he's messed up more than you are."

"The other—" He stopped suddenly. "Oh. Doesn't matter."

There it was, the little flutter in the heartbeat of the park. That secretive thing—that was the new Rattail, not the old one. The old Rattail had told me, within ten minutes of meeting me, about his father going crazy-bad and stripping all the fur off his tail. The old Rattail didn't keep secrets from me, because he didn't feel any need to. He knew he could trust me. But the new Rattail didn't seem to trust me as much anymore. Maybe he didn't trust anyone.

I didn't push it. I didn't like it, and it kind of hurt in places I couldn't wash, but I kept quiet, because what was the point of doing anything else? But I was thinking, *This is no good—I miss the Rattail I knew before that talk with Sal. How do I get him back again?*

I just kept washing his leg. Because, after all, he was still Rattail, my best friend, and he was injured and I could clean him up. At least I could do that much for him. He still trusted me that much, anyway.

"It wasn't a raccoon."

I paused and stared at him. I'd finished the injured leg and moved up, washing the fur on the thick band of muscle that bridged his shoulders. "No?"

The wound had started oozing again. "No. Dog. There's a woman with a bluetick coonhound—she was out early this morning, and she had it off its leash. Big mean thing, not very bright, and of course it went for me. That's what coonhounds do. I didn't get up the tree fast enough, I guess. I'm probably lucky I could get away at all."

His voice had risen. I wasn't saying anything, not yet. There really wasn't anything to say, because I knew that what I wanted to suggest—*let's ask Jesse to get some medicine for it, because otherwise it might fester and you could get sick and die*—wasn't going to do any good. He wasn't trusting anything on two legs, not at this point. If I even mentioned Jesse, Rattail would probably shut down again.

So I washed him, concentrating on the wound, try-ing to clean the poison out of it. I did a pretty good job, I think—when I finally stopped, it was swollen, but in a different way, more from me licking him and less from there being an infection.

Neither of us said anything much, waiting for full darkness and dinner. It was going to be another cold night; I could taste rain on the wind, just waiting to fall. From the way Rattail's nose kept twitching, I was pretty sure he did, too.

Casablanca showed up just as Jack and Angie got there. We didn't even have time to bump noses before Angie called out a greeting, and here came Sam, with Jasper in tow. Nice little party, out there on the sidewalk. At least, it would have been, if it hadn't become obvious pretty fast that Angie was furious. Not at us—she was mad about someone called Mayor.

Jasper sat, watching us eat and waiting to talk until we were a little more done. While I was working my way through my supper, I kept one ear on the conversation between the people.

". . . unbelievable." Angie was really mad. Her voice was vibrating with it, and I could smell it on her skin, like sweat. "They won't get the coyotes out of the park, but they'll push through some stupid law that says we can't feed any wild animals anywhere in the city. He's out of his tiny little mind."

"What?" Casablanca had been listening, too. "What did she say?"

"Shhh!"

I'd stopped eating. This was new, and it was bad, crazy-bad. I glanced over at Rattail, but he wasn't even looking up. It hit me, good and hard: he wasn't even surprised. He'd been expecting something, and here it was. This was the final proof for him, that he couldn't like or trust people, not anymore.

I felt something in me move, deep down, not in a good way. Even now, I don't know what it was. Maybe it was me feeling sorry that Rattail could change so much in just a few days. Maybe it was being sad because I knew that, for him, he was making a choice that felt hard and hurtful to me, and I saw him slipping away from me. One more change, in a world where all of a sudden too many things seemed to be changing too fast. When things keep shifting, moving under you like a gopher way belowground, how are you supposed to keep any control?

Sam had his jacket zipped all the way up to his chin, and Jasper had actually lowered himself all the way down to the sidewalk and was lying there, resting, hanging out. "Are you kidding? Are they nuts? I didn't see anything in the papers. What are you going to do if it passes?"

"Fight it," Angie told him. "Fight it into the ground."

Rattail had finished his pile and moved away from us. Jack went over and shook some more dry food onto the tiny remnant. "Here you go, Ratty-Rat. Of course we'll fight it, what else? And if we lose, we'll ignore it. What kind of heartless loser pulls a stunt like that?"

"Woof." Jasper had his chin on his paws; he had a sleepy look, but his eyes were wide awake. "Hey Dark, hey 'Blanca. What's up with Rattail? Is he mad at us? Because he's staying pretty far up the hillside."

"Not mad at us. Mad at the world." Casablanca met my eye for a second. She looked up and away.

Jasper had his head tilted, watching us. He was bright-eyed and friendly and just so normal, I nearly went over and washed him. "It sounds like there's been some major moves in the park. You been keeping up with what's happening to the coyote pups? They're not being left to starve, are they? Last couple of days, we've been walking out at the beach, not the park, so I'm kind of out of the loop."

I opened my mouth to fill him in, but I got a surprise: Casablanca beat me to it. She gave him the full story, all the details. She told him about Iris, the lost dog, and how Iris had taken over as the pups' protector. She even knew a few things I didn't know; I knew that Memorie was hunting to help feed the pups, but I didn't know that Memorie wasn't the only one doing the hunting for them, that she'd called in some favors.

I listened just as hard as Jasper did. Knowing something is good, knowing as much as you can is better, but what I couldn't figure out was how Casablanca knew anything at all. She was out of the park during the day, and I'd never seen any sign that she spent time around Memorie. I had a little flash, just a moment, where I got territorial and jealous about it. But I pushed that away, because really, it wasn't my business. After all, I knew how private 'Blanca was. She treasured her secrets.

A police car rolled past, and I saw the bright spotlight they have stuck on the side flash on. For a moment, I couldn't see anything, and I hate that feeling, because if I'm blinded, even for a moment, it could get me killed.

While I was trying to clear my vision, I wondered if maybe the cops wouldn't get out of the car and do something to Jack and Angie, take them away, or maybe yell at them for feeding us. But I guess this particular pair of cops were okay, because when Jack gave them a friendly wave, I saw one arm lift and wave back, and the cruiser kept rolling.

"Hey, where's Ratty?"

Angie was staring at the hillside where Rattail had been just a minute ago. He wasn't there now; during that fast little back-and-forth with the cops in the cruiser, he'd slipped away, off on whatever he was doing by himself. "I'm getting worried about that raccoon. He's been acting really strange the last few nights. And he was limping, too. Do you suppose he's been fighting with something? Another raccoon?"

Jack looked up from putting the empty cans in a paper bag. "Probably mating season. Boys will be boys, no matter what species they are. Not much we can do about it, Angie, is there? Oh, great, here comes the rain. Sam, we'll catch you later—stay warm and dry, you guys."

I watched Sam and Jasper head down the street, Sam putting the hood of his jacket up over his head. Rain was hitting the ground now, cold and loud. A

couple of drops hit me, and I flinched; for some reason, they hurt, and the memory that came into my
head was Rattail coming to tell me about the men
with the guns who had shot the two coyotes.

Casablanca had come to sit beside me. "Bet they
cut the walk short. Stupid not to. It's wet. Tree?"

"No—not yet, anyway."

Maybe I was out of my mind, but there was a need
in me, and I don't argue with those little needs, especially when they get as loud as this one was. There
was something nagging at me, right at the back of
my head, something important. I turned toward the
deep shadows of the bushes.

"I need to do something first," I told 'Blanca. "I'll
be back later."

"Okay." She wasn't heading for the tree yet herself;
she was sitting on the path, getting wet, watching me.
"Dark—about Ratty. Listen . . ."

That got my attention, all right. I stopped where I
was and waited. She seemed to be having trouble figuring out what she wanted to say. This wasn't her usual
cat-of-few-words thing; she was looking for words and
she wasn't finding them easily.

"It's—he's angry. Betrayed. What Sal told you, about how you matter to the people if you're property but not if you're wild. Raccoons aren't property. So he's angry."

I was quiet. She thought, and finally found the word she wanted. "Heartbroken. Whoa, getting wet. Later."

She went up, leaving a dry spot on the pavement where she'd been sitting. I turned and headed into the bush, being careful, heading off toward Memorie's tree. The problem was, I had no idea why I felt I needed to go, or what I was going to do when I got there.

The rain was really coming down now, a cold, wet curtain that made oncoming headlights look splintered and strange, and gave the usual noises of night in the park a steady rhythm, like a pulse. I took my time, going slowly and carefully, paying extra attention, staying mostly out of sight, only coming out in the open when I had to cross the broad grassy meadows, waiting until there was nothing coming down the road in either direction before I ran across the main street and turned toward the Children's Playground, heading for Memorie. The question that had sent me off on this little wander was still staying hidden, not letting me look at it. It was making me kind of crazy.

I turned the corner off the main drive and headed south, then stopped where I was. There it was, finally. The question, two pictures in my head, coming as clear as my own interior voice: *The pups, it's something about those pups. . . .*

Something rustled in the deep cover across the street.

It might have been anything—a Core or a coyote or just a skunk or raccoon—but I wasn't taking any chances. I looked behind me, found a tree, and went halfway up. I felt as if I were two halves of myself, doing two different things: my body was protecting itself and the rest of me, running on pure reaction, while my mind was still trying to listen to whatever was poking at it. *Those coyote pups, the orphans. Something's not right.*

It came out of the bushes, heading straight for me, fifteen feet below. It was young, not even half-grown, but it wasn't a baby, either. Not one of the orphans.

Dark, you're an idiot. The Bunker Bunny. The Dumpster. The mother teaching her pups to hunt, to

*kill, to take something apart and eat it. That was weeks
ago. Another pair of parents. Another litter of pups.*

I went up another branch, a lighter one. No way it
could climb, no way, but reaction is everything and
I wasn't taking any chances. I found a branch that
would hold my weight but not the coyote's in case I
was wrong, because wrong meant dead.

*The ones with Iris are babies. They're smaller,
younger. They're smaller now than the ones you saw
kill the Bunker Bunny were then.*

It was prowling just under me now, sniffing.
Watching, holding still, every muscle in my body
completely quiet, I saw its tongue dangle a moment,
the long dark snout brushing just over the wet grass,
picking up my scent. I heard a soft, low growl.
It lifted its head and stared up into the tree.

*There are more than one litter of coyote pups in the
park.*

Looking for me. It knew I was there. It was looking
for me.

*They're breeding. There are breeding pairs. Two
pups, four, six? How many?*

I wasn't moving, wasn't making any noise, was
barely breathing.

It couldn't see me—a black cat on a dark night is hard to find if the cat's not moving, no matter how good your eyesight is. And it couldn't climb. It was a coyote, just a kind of dog, not some kind of magical trickster-monster thing—I had to remember that. It couldn't see me. It couldn't get at me.

Go away, I thought, *just go away—you can't touch me, and I don't have to come down for anything until you're gone, so just go away and leave me alone. . . .*

Footsteps coming down the curving path behind the tree, the path leading out toward Sharon Meadow. It was very weird, because I knew those footsteps. Even through the rain, even through the wind that had sprung up and was distorting all sound, making wet leaves crackle, I knew those footsteps.

The coyote jerked its head. I saw from on high that it had beautiful ears and the stance of a hunter. I remembered that first night, sitting in Memorie's tree, admiring how beautifully nature had made her, how perfectly designed a hunter she was. Now, safe in my tree and with those footsteps about to emerge from the shadows of the path, I let myself admire that same thing in the coyote's design. It wasn't perfect—the color of its coat somehow made me think of open places with dry grass, tall and spiky and turning brown from not enough water and too much sun, nothing that worked to hide it from the eye in a green park in the middle of a city—but it was handsome, beautifully made.

The footsteps rounded the curve between the bushes, a nice easy stroll, and stopped on the path.

"Shoo."

He sounded almost amused, as if something was funny. My heart was slamming away, so hard and loud I could almost hear it.

He clapped his hands, a snap like a gunshot. "You stupid beast, I said *shoo!* Beat it. Go away."

The coyote reared back and jumped for the road. It was amazing, watching how fast it could move, how sleek it could become as it lengthened its stride. It was also scary. One move, two moves, and it was an entirely different kind of animal—different strengths. Trickster.

In the middle of the deserted road, it stopped and looked back, its eyes golden under the streetlamps. I'd been right about it; this was a very young coyote, probably one of the ones I'd seen the night I'd been penned in the Dumpster by the dog Nightmare. The size of its feet, puppy feet it had yet to grow into, gave it away.

"Shoo! Now!" His voice was a little louder, and he took a step toward it.

It fled west, into the bushes and away up the hill. I heard a distant barking, more than one dog; the coyote had probably just skirted the encampment on the hill, the group of Cores and their dogs.

"You can come down, Dark. He's gone." Jesse had come to the foot of the tree and was waiting. "I came out for some dinner. Feel like helping me eat a fish taco?"

CHAPTER FIFTEEN

When winter comes to this city, it comes as cold and rain.

I didn't have any way to compare what was happening right now with anything that came before. I'd never had to live outside before. I'd spent all my earlier winters watching the weather move down the windows, drowsing in the warm and dry. But Jesse, letting me tuck into his jacket and away from the night and the weather, made a comparison of his own.

"Long cold winter ahead. It's going to be a tough one, if it's already this cold and raining this hard. One of the worst I've seen." He felt me settle in and zipped the jacket up.

Life and death in the park might be normal, but

you can't convince me that anyone on the receiving end of the death thing doesn't get spooked about it. I was tight, and still shaky, and I couldn't seem to stop talking, for some reason. I poked my head out of the jacket and stared up into his face. "That was a coyote. A young coyote. One of the ones I saw eating the Bunker Bunny. It wanted to catch me. It wanted to kill me."

He peered down at me. The jacket had a hood, and he pulled it up over his head, framing his face with fleecy wool. "Yep. It did. Good thing I was around— pretty easy for me to scare it away. After all, it's really just a dog, when you think about it. By themselves, coyotes are pretty shy about coming near people— that's what I've heard, anyway. I don't seem to be able to understand them. Not sure why—maybe they're just not interested in communicating."

"I want them to go away. Long cold winter and hard rain—isn't that going to be bad enough without a park full of coyotes chasing me? Why won't anyone make them go away?"

He tickled the top of my head, right between the ears, and I felt myself begin to purr. "Well, I'll do my best.

So long as it's just one or two, I can always get them to split. Don't know how much longer it's just going to be one or two, though. We may have a problem."

"What do you mean? Did something happen?" There had been something in his voice; it was weird, how fast I could pick up on his changes, on his moods.

We were walking, or at least he was, not toward Memorie's tree but back toward my usual territory. "Something I saw. I stayed at my mother's house last night. My father's in the hospital, and she wanted some company. She gets a little spooked when she has to be by herself too long—it's a really big house and she's not used to being alone. As long as my father's not there, I'm good with being there."

A few drops of rain hit me in the nose, and I hunkered down a little deeper. "Hospital?"

"Yep. It's a place where they take people who get sick. Turns out my father's sick. I only just found out."

"Oh." I remembered what he'd said about his father, how his father was mean, how he didn't like him. "Should I say I'm sorry? That he's sick, I mean?"

"Not unless you're actually sorry, no." His voice didn't change, not at all, but his heartbeat did—it sped up for a few seconds, then settled down to normal again. Pressed up against his chest, I could feel it. "But anyway, their house? It's up on the hill, Ashbury Heights. Yeah, I know, you don't know where that is. It's southeast of here. And when I was walking over last night, I saw coyotes."

He stopped for a moment, stopped walking, stopped talking. We were under a streetlamp and he was looking down at me. It occurred to me that he was waiting for me to respond to him. It took a second or two, because I was processing.

"Coyotes? You mean more than one?"

"Four. Together. They were crossing Frederick Street. Heading out into the Haight. Hey! Ouch! Mind the claws, please."

"Sorry."

I'd flexed them, digging in. No way to help it. What he'd said, that was scary, a whole new level of scary-bad, the kind that brings out my weapons. "Four. Together? You mean they were in a pack?"

"Yes. You know what really freaked me out, though? They weren't afraid of me, Dark, not at all. They didn't run or even back off. Just the opposite—they paced me, for the better part of two blocks. Hell, the only reason they finally went the other way was because some guy on a motorcycle came down the street, and I guess the noise made them decide they wanted to be elsewhere. But they weren't afraid of me. They weren't afraid of anything."

"What—?" I stopped, realizing that my fur was standing up along the ridge of my spine. "What were they doing?"

"Hunting."

If I hadn't been freaked before, I was now. I remembered the shreds of bloodied fur in the Rose Garden, all that had been left of the Red Father. I remembered the slow stripping apart of the Bunker Bunny. I thought about the young coyote under my tree, knowing I was there, wanting me, waiting: its shoulders, the set of its tail, its long nose pointed up toward me, black and velvety and wet. Scenting me . . .

I guess he must have felt me tense up, because I was pretty sure I hadn't made any noise. "It's okay. All right, maybe it's not okay. But it's okay right now, Dark, right this second. So, um, could you sheathe the claws, please? You're kind of pointy."

I took a breath and forced myself to relax. He was right: for the moment, I was as safe as it could get, tucked inside his jacket.

"Sorry," I told him, but it wasn't strictly true. No one in their right mind is sorry to have a way to protect themselves. "Jesse, do you know someone called Mayor?"

"You could say so, yes. What a weird question. Why?"

I thought back, to how angry Angie had been. It was funny, but I liked her anger. It felt right to me. "Because he says no one's allowed to feed us anymore. That's what Jack and Angie Warm said, anyway—the people who feed us. Why would he want to do that? Do you know?"

"Oh, for—!" We'd stopped again; he sounded exasperated. "I swear to God, people are so stupid some days, I'm ashamed to be human. Look, Dark, can you tell me what you remember? As close to what they actually said as possible."

I thought about it for minute and gave him everything I could think of, as close to how the people had said it as I could. He listened, not interrupting or asking any questions, but a couple of times, I thought he was rolling his eyes.

". . . and Angie was really mad," I finished. "I don't know what half that stuff was, that she told Sam she wouldn't mind doing to this Mayor guy for being such a jerk, but they didn't sound like fun to me. What's 'drawing and quartering' mean?"

"Something seriously nasty." He still sounded exasperated, but now there was something else in there. Appreciation? Like maybe he liked some of Angie's ideas. "Let's just say it's a very messy way to die. Yeah, she sounds royally ticked off, and I don't blame her. I can check on that tomorrow—I know a lot of people down at City Hall. That's where the guy called Mayor hangs out. It's also where my father hangs out."

"I thought you said he was hanging out in a hospital?"

We were walking again. Jesse's shoes were making big wet squelchy noises, slapping against the puddles on the sidewalk, sending spray everywhere.

"Not because he wants to be, that's for sure. Having some expert sticking tubes in him—and needles and stuff—not so much. And having doctors ordering him to bend over, or cough, or stop squirming—that's just the kind of thing to send my dear dad right into full flip-out mode. He's a major control freak. He doesn't like listening to other experts anyway, because he doesn't believe they exist. He doesn't get a vote right now, though. Not much choice. You can't just cite a tumor for contempt of court, bang a gavel, and throw it in jail for a month because it won't cooperate with you. I guess he's finding that out the hard way."

I stayed quiet. I didn't really get what he was talking about, but I didn't have to, really, because the actual words didn't matter. It was the tone of voice I understood, the change in how warm his skin was and the way his heart changed the way it was beating. That much I already knew about him: those things happened just that way only when he was talking about his father.

The jacket had nice deep pockets, and he had his hands warm inside, supporting my weight. "I'll call over to City Hall in the morning. Sounds to me like someone down there decided they were getting too much negative press about that shooting. So of course the way they deal with it is to sneak some idiotic legislation through without telling anyone until it's official. Or maybe Mister Mayor feels the need to kiss up to the animal-rights crazies, or maybe someone downtown owes the boys at Park and Rec a favor—they aren't nuts about most of the animals in the park. But either way, you don't need to worry, Dark. This kind of law doesn't usually apply to feral cats."

"It doesn't? Why not?" Still no real clue what he was talking about, but I was beginning to just make sense of it.

"Because you're not wild animals." Jesse had a knack for good, clear explanations. "Cats are something else, legally. You're domestic pets. It's just that some of you get treated like crap by the humans around you, and you end up having to live on your own, so you end up having to share your food with the skunks and raccoons."

"But raccoons are wild animals, right? Legally? Not good. Are you sure, Jesse?"

He stopped again. This was turning into one of the most stop-and-start walks we'd taken. "No, but I will be, once I call in. Why isn't it good?"

"Because this is going to give Rattail one more

reason to not trust anyone or anything. Jesse, he's already different than he was. Ever since Sal told us why those men shot the two coyotes, Ratty's been feeling—I don't know—like he's been betrayed, like trusting anyone is dangerous and dumb. This is just going to make it worse. And I don't want it to be worse. I want him back the way he was."

I could see just what was going to happen, when he found out that I could get fed, Casablanca could get fed, but he couldn't, not without the Warms breaking some stupid law.

He thought about it for a moment. "Ouch. I see what you mean. And it won't change anything if he knows that Jack and Angie Whatsis—what did you call them? The Warms? Is that their last name? Anyway, that they're going to keep feeding him and not caring about the law. Because he's still going to feel like a second-class citizen. That's the problem, isn't it?"

"I guess, except I don't know what a second-class—whoa! What was *that*?"

It was a bad noise, a sad noise, a scary noise; it came from everywhere, anywhere, cutting through the sound of the rain with no trouble at all. First the squeal of something that sounded like a car, then a really hard thump, then the squeal of something else, and at the end of it all, that noise, a wail, a howl.

Fear, loss, pain, something. Scary-bad.

I couldn't be sure where it had come from; I couldn't be sure whether one or both of those squeals had come from something alive or not. I couldn't imagine what was wailing.

I guess Jesse had a better sense of direction in the rain than I did. Or maybe it was just that, all stuffed down inside his jacket like that, I couldn't really get the sense of where everything really was. But Jesse began to run, me still inside his coat, bouncing up and down as his feet pounded against the pavement, heading back the way we'd come, down toward Memorie's tree and the carousel.

It was really strange. I didn't feel as if I had control over anything I was doing, but I managed to get my head up and out. All I saw was the rain beating down. The park was basically empty, no people and no cars, except some red taillights off in the distance, all the way down the road toward where Iris had the pups stashed in their lair.

And then we turned the corner where a spur in the road leads down to the carousel, and everything changed—the whole picture was different.

Jesse stopped running, and I got my eyes to work. That noise was coming from just beyond the curve, a terrible heartbreaking noise, the sound you might expect to hear if the entire world was made of sorry.

"Oh, man. Oh, man." Jesse was still now, very still, not moving at all. There wasn't any reason for him to move, because there was nothing he could do.

The dog Iris had lost the remnants of the leash she'd snapped when she bolted away into the park, so many days ago. The collar was still there, a thin dark line, hanging loose around the base of her throat. It looked as if a piece of the night had found her and attached itself to her, that dark line, as she stretched her face to the sky and wept, a long, sobbing howl that bounced off the rain and the wind and the trees and came back down again.

Looking down, I could tell that whoever had been driving the car hadn't stopped. They'd skidded, leaving long black rubbery-looking smears on the ground. So maybe they'd tried to stop, but they hadn't. They hadn't hung around to check up on the damage done, either.

The coyote pup had probably died right away; from the look of it, the car's tires had hit it and gone right over it. No suffering or pain, just here and then gone, leaving a littermate to wonder and a mother who wasn't really a mother to grieve. The other pup was nowhere in sight.

"Jesus." Jesse was speaking quietly, but really, I don't think it would made any difference; the dog Iris was so deep into her grief, she had no room in her eyes for Jesse or anything else. And anyway, her sobbing drowned him out. "Man, this sucks. Poor baby. At least he never knew what hit him—dying fast, I'd rather go that way myself. People drive way too fast in this park."

The dog Iris looked up then. I saw her register Jesse standing there, saw the realization in her face—*human people, human dangerous, will hurt me, people always hurt me, human dangerous, run away.* Her front legs, short and muscled with thin yellow fur, tensed for a jump that would take her fleeing through the bushes, to where he couldn't get near her. But I saw as the second realization hit her, too—*one baby left, can't run, can't go, protect, protect, can't help this one but the other, protect, protect* . . . I saw her head jerk around, desperate to find the second pup.

"It's okay."

Jesse was easy, calm, not moving. There was nothing in his voice to scare Iris or anything else; I remembered that he'd said he could talk with dogs. Early the dog had understood him perfectly. I wondered if Iris did, too.

"The other pup's in the bush behind you. Get him home safe, okay? And get yourself home safe, too. You ready, Dark? Let's head out."

He turned away, not looking back. As we reached the fork where the spur road emptied into the road west, I heard a frightened whimpering behind us, back in the darkness we'd just left: the surviving pup had come out, looking for Iris the dog, for the mother who wasn't, for the keeper of comfort, to lead it home.

CHAPTER SIXTEEN

Winter, and changes came in with the season.

The day, my time to sleep, got shorter, while the nights, my time to prowl, got longer. New routines began to take shape, and it wasn't just because of the long hours without sun or crowds of people. It had to do with other things, too: for one thing, Jesse was coming around a lot more than he had before, and that meant I was getting a lot more time snuggled down in his jacket, out of the rain. I still hung out in my tree, and I still ate with Casablanca and Rattail most every night. But when Jesse was around, I found myself hanging with him. It felt good. It felt right.

Casablanca wasn't around as much as she had been. When the rains really began, she'd show up just before dinner, but instead of the good-weather routine of staying in the park after we ate, she'd head straight out for the garage in her old house. She asked me a couple of times if I wanted to come along, spend the night out of the cold and wet. I appreciated her asking me, letting me know that her turf was open to me, but the timing was wrong; both times she asked, Jesse showed up, and I went with him instead.

So I was about as safe as any of us living in the park could be, because the need to hunt was cut way down. And I didn't even have to feel too guilty about it, because 'Blanca had Rattail with her most of the time. They were keeping each other company. That was a good thing, because I was worried about both of them. If they were together, being each other's eyes and ears against the winter and whatever walked in it, then they were that much safer and I didn't have to worry as much. And part of me was really worried about Rattail, because the place on his leg where the dog had hurt him wasn't healing too well. The infection had gone away—I think my washing had helped that—but the leg was weak. He was slower now.

Ratty himself was different, too. That change in

him, the cautious untrusting thing, seemed to have
settled into him, under the skin. It was part of him
now. He'd become angry, careful in a way that made
me ache inside somewhere.

He still let me wash him, just like before, back
when he was still acting like my very best friend, but
there was something fierce in him now. He always
seemed to be keeping his distance from me, especially when Jesse was around. It took me too long to
figure that part of it out; I trusted Jesse, Rattail didn't.
He wasn't going to trust another human being again,
not ever. And that meant that he wasn't going to let
me get close, not the way he had before. It felt as if
he wanted to make me choose: him or Jesse. And I
wasn't going to choose, because it wasn't fair—it was
dumb—and why should I have to do that?

I couldn't let my attention stay there, though. And I
didn't know whether the news about what happened
to Iris's pup was all over the park or not, but I couldn't
worry about that, either. Now that the coyotes were
here, those of us who made the night our time weren't
just hunting. We were being hunted.

One night, about a week after the pup had been

killed by the car, Jesse showed up at my tree. It was early for him, and it was the first time he'd done that while Jack and Angie were still there.

He just strolled down the path while we were eating, and Jack and Angie were standing there shivering, making sure all three of us got our dinner without any trouble from anyone. Ratty was up on the grassy part of the hill, as usual, so he wasn't anywhere near Jesse. But Casablanca and I were right in his way, and neither of us was going anywhere.

"Um . . . excuse me, but please be careful. There are some of the park animals eating here." Angie was polite, but she didn't sound as if she was going to take no for an answer. She was a strange woman; it didn't take much to make her mad, but when she did get mad, it seemed to make her want to protect things.

"I know. Don't worry—they're old friends of mine." He sounded mellow, very easy and unthreatening. "Hey Casablanca, hey Dark. Boy, it's cold out here tonight. Glad to see the kitties are getting a good meal. And is that a raccoon chowing down up there on the hillside . . . ?"

Of course, that led to a nice friendly conversation.

The fact that he knew both our names, that 'Blanca didn't even bother to stop chewing, much less run, the fact that I stopped eating long enough to bump his ankles and say hello, seemed to reassure both the Warms. They got into one of those weird little conversations, where everyone jumps from subject to subject and no one sticks to anything, but then it all goes in a circle and they wind up talking about whatever it was they started out with in the first place. People are very strange.

So we munched away, the people talked, and then, out of nowhere, a police cruiser came up alongside and turned one of those stupid bright spots they like so much right at us. It was a different color car this time, all white instead of black and white. Jesse didn't seem too concerned, but of course, now that I knew that his father was someone the police had to be careful about, I knew why he didn't care much about what they thought or did. Angie and Jack, though, that was different.

Angie had turned her head toward the cruiser. She was speaking loud, and very clear.

"Would you mind getting that light out of everyone's

eyes? It's unnecessary, it's annoying, and if you dam-age my eyesight, you'll be getting a bill, believe me."

The light turned off, and one of the cops rolled down the window. "What are you folks doing out here?"

"Exactly what it looks like. Same thing we've done every night for the past seven years or so: feeding the cats." Jack didn't sound much friendlier than Angie did. And it was kind of a stupid question.

"You shouldn't be feeding them." The cop didn't sound friendly, either. "The mayor recently passed a new law—"

"We know all about it." Angie was really getting mad now. She took a step toward the cruiser and made sure her voice was right in their faces.

"There's a new law that prohibits feeding wild ani-mals," she snapped. "Feral cats are not considered wild animals, under any legal classification. Go look it up before you start issuing little orders and making little announcements. And by the way, do me a favor and tell the mayor he can kiss my butt. He pushed this garbage through behind closed doors. I have every intention of rubbing his face in it, especially since he hasn't done a thing about controlling the coyotes."

"Look, lady, I'm not the one who—"

Jesse broke in. He sounded about as bored as it's possible to get. "Yo, officers? Those are cats. They're not wild animals, they're domestic animals who happen to be homeless. Some of them got dumped out here by stupid people. The occasional raccoon comes over and gets given a mouthful, just to keep it away from hassling the cats. The TNR program has been around since long before you guys ever watched *NYPD Blue* or got the hots for playing with guns, or whatever made you want to do this for a living. It's useful, necessary, and sanctioned. Now get a grip, go catch a criminal or something, maybe bully a few homeless kids. And have a nice night."

Of course, that got them mad. The tone in the cop's voice when he demanded "to see a little ID" made me think that if he'd had a gun, he might have just taken a shot at Jesse. And the tone wasn't lost on Angie and Jack, either. Angie was boiling mad; if the cop sounded like he wanted to shoot, Angie made it clear that what she really wanted to do was pull both cops out of their car and hit them over the head with it.

By this time, I'd finished eating, and so had 'Blanca. She lifted her head at me, washed her face, muttered, "This could get messy, out of here, bye," and headed north, toward Fulton Street and the shelter of her old garage. Ratty was still sitting in the grass. He wasn't watching the people—he was watching me, waiting to see what I was going to do.

Right that moment, I wasn't planning to do anything, and I couldn't figure out why he thought I would want to get in on anything. This was all people stuff, people business. Even if it had to do with the cats or the coons or anything else that lived in the park, what was I supposed to be doing about it, except watching and listening and learning what I had to know to keep me alive? All I really wanted to do right then was wash my face, and that's what I did.

Jesse actually got to the police cruiser before Angie and Jack did. He flipped open the little leather envelope he always carried with him and handed it to the cop who'd been doing all the talking. Something about the way he was moving or standing—maybe just how completely not worried he was—convinced Angie to stand back and let him go first. She's usually so fierce, I expected her to get up in the cop's face, but she didn't.

"Brangolder-Wyse? The DA? Any relation?" Of course the cop knew the name; I could tell. So did the Warms. You could see it in the way Jack's head whipped around, the way he and Angie were staring at Jesse.

"My father."

If I'd had any doubt about it, those two words cleared it up. Jesse really didn't care. He didn't care what the cop thought, he didn't care what stupid law that Mayor guy passed, he just didn't care about any of this stuff. It didn't matter to him—he hung out in the park because he wanted to, he hung out with the cats and the dogs because he wanted to, he went home and visited his mother because he wanted to. It was all about that: he wanted to do something, so he did it.

So it was pretty lucky that, as far as I could tell, he didn't want to do things that would hurt anyone else, except maybe his father. The way he dealt with his father in his own head, that was muffled and messy.

But basically, he was about as free as a human

could get. I suddenly found myself wondering what it was like to be that free and have all the power that comes with being a human being, too. I mean, I'm pretty free—the only thing that makes me have to do anything I don't want to do is the whole having-to-stay-alive thing. But Jesse was free, and he had all the power. That gave me a very clear moment, where I understood just why Ratty was so angry and resentful, and it wasn't a good feeling.

These people decided if we could live or die. They decided if we could have babies, if we could eat. They had trucks that only had one purpose, to catch us and take us away if we didn't "belong" to some other human being. I didn't know what they did with animals they caught that way. I didn't think I wanted to know; I just wanted to make really sure that they didn't catch me or any of my friends.

All that power, and freedom, too. It seemed, I don't know, like maybe Jesse had been given too much somehow. For a scary moment, I got why Rattail was becoming the way he was now. There doesn't seem to be enough balance in the world.

"I heard your father was taking some time off." The

cop still didn't sound too friendly. "That's what the paper said, anyway. What did he do, tick someone off once too often?"

"Why don't you ask him yourself?"

Jesse had gone chilly, a voice I hadn't heard coming out of him before: hard, sarcastic, almost mean. You could almost hear the cop's mouth zip itself shut, the breath whistling through his nostrils. Jesse kept talking in that same voice.

"Ask him who he ticked off, I mean. Then you can tell him why you think it's any of your business. I'd love to watch that. I'll even set it up for you. I'll hook you up with him. What's your name, Officer? What station are you out of?"

After that, of course, they didn't check Jack's and Angie's IDs. The cruiser pulled away so hard and fast, it left a nasty smell in the air, kind of like the tires were on fire.

Jack was still looking at Jesse. He was grinning and doing something only people seem to be able to do: lifting one eyebrow and leaving the other one right where it was. I think it looks really funny, and anyway, they don't all seem to be able to do it. Angie didn't look as happy as Jack did—I got the feeling she'd really wanted to get into a fight with the cops.

"Nice," Jack told him. "That was beyond impressive and all the way into fantastic. Did I get that right? You're Robert Brangolder-Wyse's son? Because that was a nifty way to handle those cops. The guy looked like he'd just been smacked across the face with a big, wet, stinky fish. A dead, wet, stinky fish." He laughed suddenly. "Man, way to get them to knock off the power-tripping!"

"Yeah. Nice to know my father's good for something. Don't see why mine should be the only life he gets to make miserable." Jesse looked down at me. "Wow, this rain's not kidding, is it? Looks like Casablanca has headed off for dryer digs. Hey, Dark, you want a ride—whoa!"

I'd jumped for his chest before he actually got the zipper to his jacket open for me, so of course I landed wrong, claws out, grabbing on to the coat, hanging on. He staggered back under the impact, laughed, and got one arm under me.

"Hey, slide over, okay? I need to—okay, never mind. Climb on in. Silly cat."

He pulled the zipper up over me. Warm in there, and dry, and familiar. I settled in, looking out.

"Wow." Angie was looking at me, with her mouth open. She was really wet and getting wetter every minute, but for the moment, she didn't seem to notice. "That's incredible! Would you look at her? She must really like you. We've been feeding her every night since she got here, and she'll maybe bump my ankles once in a while. But if I tried to pick her up, she'd be ten feet away in a tenth of a second. How did you convince her to let you carry her around? Did you smear your underwear with catnip or something?"

Jesse scratched me between the ears, and of course, I started a loud, rattling purr. I can't help purring when anyone does that. "I guess I just speak her language. Hey, Dark, let's wander. You may have eaten, but I haven't had any dinner yet, and I'm hungry. Jack, Angie, nice to meet you—and stay dry. See you later."

We'd actually walked for a couple of minutes before I realized why things felt different: we were going the opposite way from Jesse's usual route. Normally, we'd be heading toward the Haight-Ashbury, the area to the south and east of the park; his mother's house was that way, and there were shops and restaurants and places he could get stuff he wanted. I'd been out of the park with him a few times now, and we'd always gone that way.

But tonight, we were heading toward what had been my own tree, before I'd switched to the one by the feeding spot. I saw the outline of the back of the museum tower, the funny, curvy lights that look sort of like birds with long necks leading up to the complex, the streetlights out on Fulton Street to the north close enough to count.

"Jesse? Are we going the wrong way? Or are we going somewhere special?"

"Yeah, just for a few minutes."

We'd reached the little bridge at Tenth Avenue. Rattail had told me that it was new, part of what they'd done to rebuild the museum, that there was a whole garage underneath it now where hundreds of people could park their cars if they wanted to wander. It spans JFK Drive, and there's a raceway behind the trees next to it.

I'd been over it plenty of times, back when I was first dumped and I decided to migrate east from the beach and the buffalo paddocks, but I didn't come down here much anymore. I really hadn't liked it too much since the night we saw the first coyote. Something about that memory—the burning shopping cart, the shreds of bloodied fur that had once been the Red Father in the Rose Garden, and the coyote trotting out of the mist and looking at me and Ratty with cold empty eyes—had pretty much soured that part of the park for me. It felt like danger to me. It felt like trouble.

"There's something I want to check out. Let's just hang out here for a little while, and if nothing happens, we'll head back out the other way, okay?"

Jesse took a few steps farther east, away from the lights on the museum walkway, down toward the long service entry for the museum itself, the big meadow next to it, and down toward the shadows where the road curves west. For some reason, even though I was safe in his jacket and hearing his heart beating steadily away against me, I was still tense, a little spooked. Every instinct I had was yelling at me, signaling loud and clear: *danger, red alert, eyes open, danger.*

So I really wasn't all that surprised when the three coyotes came out from behind the big Dumpster the museum keeps in the meadow. Scared, yes, but not really surprised.

They came across the grass, moving with that not-quite run I'd seen the other coyotes use: not fast, sort of a dancy, loping thing. What did surprise me was how they seemed almost as if they'd used some kind of magic, or maybe trickery, to get here. One moment there hadn't been anything there; the next moment, they'd materialized out of the wet grass and the line of bushes. For some reason, I thought of Sal, the way the bundle of rags would suddenly become someone speaking to me, and how I'd jump every time. Ghosts and tricksters.

I pushed down inside the jacket, watching the coyotes. Only my face and whiskers and ears were out there. I ignored the rain pelting down, ignored anything that wasn't the coyotes. I watched them, concentrating, eyes fixed.

This had to be what Jesse had been looking for— the coyotes right here in this one spot—but I still didn't know what he expected them to do, or if I was supposed to be watching for something, too.

They were halfway across the road when they

stopped. One of them turned, capered, lifted his nose to the sky; the other two came out into the road, looking around, careful and cautious.

The smallest of the three, probably a female, circled the other two. They touched noses, rubbing their muzzles against one another. There was something nice about it, a kind of tenderness in the way they were acting. It looked like they were dancing, the way the Red Father had danced with his family at the other end of this road, so many weeks ago.

But Red Father was dead, and so were the rest of the foxes. Those memories, the dancing foxes and the bloody fur on the grass, stabbed at me. I remembered the Red Father, how he'd met my eye from five feet away, and it hurt. He'd known I was no threat to his babies, and he'd let me know that so long as that was true, he was no threat to me.

And now he was gone. Too much was lost, too much had happened, too many changes. Nothing good for me ever seems to come from change.

Those coyotes, dancing out in the middle of the road on a night with driving rain and no moon, one of them might have been the one who killed the Red

Father. I couldn't tell. They were beautiful and they were dangerous—to me, and to anything in the park they thought was food or competition.

Jesse took a step backward, then another. His heart rate had stayed the same the entire time.

The movement caught the coyotes' attention. They stopped, going very still, heads turning. I didn't know if they could see me—I don't know anything about how well dogs can see, if they're about smell and hearing instead of vision.

But they saw Jesse. And they weren't scared.

I was, though. The voice in my head, the instinct voice, was suddenly talking at me again, good and loud: *Three of them and only one Jesse, what if they jump him, they could surround him and bring him down if they wanted to, we're outnumbered, three of them.*

I don't know how long we stayed like that, but it felt like forever. The coyotes looked at Jesse, three pairs of eyes gleaming out at him. I saw them considering it, wondering: *Could we take him down, would he resist or would he be an easy kill?* And for the first time, I felt Jesse's body temperature change, felt his heart rate begin to climb. . . .

A sudden rush of sound from the trees to the north of us. A shadow of an owl's long wings, a sharp angry call from a voice I knew, warning them: *On your way!*

She came down low, dangerously low, wings cutting through the rain, steel feet wet and shining. She came down so low, I thought for a second that she might try to take one. The picture was there, superimposing itself between real and my mind: the owl grabbing with her talons, lifting the coyote off the ground, the coyote howling.

Then the picture was gone and so was Memorie, back up into the canopy. She was far from her own tree, but maybe she was out hunting food for Iris and the remaining pup.

Yellow lights, heading east on JFK Drive, cut through the mist and the falling water. The coyotes were gone, moving fast as Memorie warned them off, jumping to the north side of the road. Jesse was breathing normally again; he turned his body, and me with it, to watch them go. The streetlamps on Fulton Street caught their silhouettes as they hit the raceway and left the park for the streets of the city.

CHAPTER SEVENTEEN

I was so used to seeing Jesse every day that when five stormy days went by without any sign of him in the park, I started worrying. The problem was, there was nothing I could do about it. And there wasn't anyone to talk to about it, either.

"I wish the rain would go away. I'm sick of being wet all the time."

The words cut through the nice little nap I'd been having. I lifted my head off my front paws and looked at Rattail, who'd climbed back up to hang out with me for the afternoon. He sounded cranky, peevish, and it wasn't hard to see why; the rain had been falling since late last night, a steady, dreary curtain of water. It wasn't a storm, not really—there was no real wind, just little gusts, so at least it wasn't too cold. No wind meant it was safer to stay in the trees. But it was still nasty and gray, and even climbing down to stretch or go to the bathroom was no fun.

Curled up on my own branch of the three that forked out from the main trunk, I was close enough to wash Ratty's face. I thought about it for a moment; the old Ratty, I'd have just held him down and licked like crazy, but these last few weeks, the way he'd been changing, I never knew how he would react, and I was afraid to try.

Today, though, it was almost like having my friend back the way he used to be, and I decided to just do it. The worst he could do was tell me to stop.

"How's your leg?"

"My—oh, the bite? Better. I'm still kind of slow, though—the muscle isn't working right yet. I think it's going to heal okay, but it's taking too long. I need to be able to *ru*-un."

He had his eyes closed, and I washed the cheek closest to me. His fur tasted just like the park—my tongue was picking up dampness and dust and other things I couldn't quite identify. I paused, sniffing; other animal scents were there, very faintly, and something very familiar that I couldn't place. Whatever it was, it made me think of being inside a house.

He shifted his weight in the crook of the branch, and I caught an actual smell of that same unidentified-house thing coming off his fur. "You really ought to come to 'Blanca's with us. There's a pile of old blankets in the garage. We've been sleeping on those, and they're really warm and soft. Did I say something funny?"

"No."

I had it now, the memory, the people putting my fleecy cat bed in the washing machine, taking it out, putting it in the dryer and tossing in a sheet of some kind of paper with it. This was that same not-quite-sweet smell.

Ratty was looking at me, waiting, and I tried to explain.

"I don't really want to, Ratty. I know she's okay with it. She keeps asking me to come along. But it's not my turf. And it's not just that it isn't my turf, it's that it isn't really Casablanca's turf, either. She doesn't really have a home there anymore—she's just sneaking in. I know it gets nasty out here, the coyotes and the cold and people who let their dogs run loose and stuff. And I know this is just a tree, not as good as a house. But this is *mine*. I can be in it, and no one and nothing can tell me I have to leave. And if someone does, I have the right to fight back."

He looked at me, and I looked right back at him. The rain dripped down through the treetops, branches stark and twisted against the sky—the canopy was missing half its leaves, stripped by the winter winds. Somewhere in my head was a picture of the inside of Jesse's fleecy coat, resting there, warm and dry and safe.

For a moment, I was dizzy. Dizzy isn't a good thing to be, not when you're a cat, and even if you're not a cat, dizzy when you're halfway up a tree is also not too good. I dug my claws in hard, feeling the branch under me, rough bark, water slipping down the tree to the ground below . . .

"Are you okay?" Ratty sounded worried, just the way he used to sound. "Because, you know what— you're swaying back and forth. That doesn't look too safe. Dark?"

"I'm fine. I think I got some rainwater in my ear, that's all." I wasn't fine, not really, but I wasn't about to tell him that. I wasn't going to tell him why, either. It felt so nice to have Ratty back again, even if it was just for right now. And I knew that, if I even mentioned Jesse, it was going to mess things up, make him close up again.

Ratty turned around and presented me with the sore leg to wash. "Oh, good. Here, take a look at that bite. Does it look as if it's getting better?"

"Not too bad." I sniffed; it smelled clean enough, no infection, but it was still puffy. "It—*Ratty*!"

Noise, a loud terrifying *crack* that echoed up and down, and then suddenly I wasn't dizzy anymore, because the branch Ratty had been sitting on wasn't there under him anymore, and he was falling, crashing down through the smaller lighter branches. There was a pale jagged gash in the crook of the tree; it had sheared completely off under his weight.

"Ratty! Ratty?"

"I'm okay. Stupid tree. Stupid branch. Stupid rain." I heard him coming back up.

"What happened?" It was a dumb question, and I knew that as soon as I asked it. It was pretty obvious what had happened: we'd been getting a lot of rain, and the water gets into the trees and soaks through, weakening the tree. It wasn't just the branches, either; the roots were soaked with water, too, and some of the trees had come crashing down entirely. Wandering around the park with Jesse, he'd told me about a couple of bad winters, when the winds had howled for days and trees had come crashing down all over the park. The big glass Conservatory, where they kept the flowers, that had been trashed by the wind and rain. I could see the fancy, funny glass roof through the trees and bushes, right from my own tree. It had taken them years to rebuild it.

Anyway, he was halfway back up the tree before I thought, *Wow, he's really making a lot of noise*, and right after that, I realized he wasn't the only one climbing. There was something climbing up behind him. I could hear it, nice and clear: two sets of scrabbling claws or feet. I tensed up, wondering if I was going to have to bite something to get rid of it—after all, Ratty still had a bad leg.

But it was okay, because first there was Ratty's head and then his front legs, pulling up onto the branch next to mine. I'd been right about there being someone else coming up, because a moment later, something small and green and round popped up right next to me.

"Sal!"

"Well, looky, here's a babycat. How's my girl?" She reached out, one small hand, and touched my shoulder. It was funny; I hadn't really noticed her hands before. She was wearing knit gloves with the finger parts mostly cut off. I could see her knuckles, bumpy and thick, pressing up against the knit gloves.

I was up on all fours, arching my back, balancing on the slippery bark. I head-butted her, rubbing my cheek against her arm; she smelled even more like the park than Ratty did, and there was no fabric-softener smell on her, either. I suddenly remembered how, the night I met her, she'd told me to fly and I'd understood then that she was part of the park, part of the earth, that she was never going to fly and that was probably why she'd wanted me to.

"Sal, what are you doing here? Is something happening? And how'd you get up the tree, in all those things you're wearing?"

It was a serious question. I don't usually pay a lot of

attention to what people wear, and Sal always seemed to be covered up, head to toe, in layers of things that made her look like a bundle of laundry someone had forgotten about. I understood that it was more than just keeping warm; this was her way of camouflaging, of self-protecting and being left alone.

Maybe it was because that branch crashing down—and taking Rattail with it—had sharpened me up. Whatever it was, I looked at her, curled up no bigger than a child, and I saw a lot more rags on her than I'd ever seen before. Even her feet were wrapped up in them; all I could see were the tips of the cracked, old, oversized men's shoes she always wore, because the rest of the shoes were wrapped up in battered, dirty green fabric.

"Maybe I fly up here, just like I told you to. Hey, raccoon, you come up here and sit with me. Branch be dry—ain't goin' nowhere. Come on up."

She was sitting on Casablanca's usual branch. Using this tree as our regular perch was going to need rethinking, because there were three of us, usually, and now only two branches. Ratty edged up, and hunkered down. Funny, he didn't trust humans anymore—he'd said so and he showed it—but he didn't seem to have any problem with Sal. Maybe it was because she smelled right to him.

"You know one of them coyote pups got hit by a car." It wasn't a question, it was a statement. She knew we knew, but I nodded anyway.

"Good," she told us. "And you know that girl Iris be watching the other pup night and day. There's other stuff you ain't been told about yet. Other stuff you ain't found out, stuff come home to you. You ought to know, so I come up."

I was staring at her, all my nerves tingling. My fur wanted to lift and I let it, rippling up along my spine. I was pretty sure that, if Sal had taken the trouble to come up here and tell us something, it was something we were going to need to know.

Rattail's nose was quivering, and he was showing his teeth. "Is it that the coyotes are hunting outside the park? Because we knew that. We've seen them, me and Casablanca, going into yards along Fulton Street. And we know about them hunting in packs. Memorie told us, too. We knew that."

"Ain't about that." Her eyes looked straight at me,

and I suddenly wished, hard and deep and aching, that I was asleep somewhere warm, that Sal's voice was walking me through long sweet dreams of Bastet in her royal city, instead of being wide awake, scared in a tree, with her voice about to give me some bad news. Because it was bad news. I could feel it. And I wanted to hear it and get it over with.

"Sal? Just tell us, please."

"It's something happening right now, right this second."

She jerked her head out and down toward JFK Drive, just as a lot of police cars, a whole line of them, came roaring down the street, heading east. There were some black-and-whites, and some of the white park ranger cars. Whatever they were doing and wherever they were heading, they were going there fast.

She spoke again, and this time, her voice had no feeling in it at all. She really sounded like Memorie for a second.

"They gonna sweep the homeless. Kids you call the Cores. Mayor says it's all the Cores' fault the coyotes came here—says the camps are dirty, that the coyotes stick around because they can steal food and scavenge from the dirty camps. So first he pass a law says no one can feed anything, then he tell the police, you go sweep them dirty homeless people right out of the park. Then folks shut up about them coyotes, maybe. Nobody be feeding nothin', maybe the coyote problem solve itself. That man, he's stupid as a bag of hair."

I looked at Rattail, and he looked back. We had the same thought in both our minds—I could see it. Ratty got ready to hit the ground, getting into position to slide butt-first down the tree. It would be evening soon, and anyway the weather was bad, so going halfway across the park in daytime wasn't as tricky as it could have been on a nice day. There weren't that many people out today, and we knew how to be careful of cars. "We need to go see. Do you know where, Sal?"

"Sharon Meadow, right next to the carousel. Police be rounding everyone up. You watch how you go, now."

Those black bottomless eyes didn't seem to be blinking. As if she'd caught at my thought, she let her eyelids droop, just for a moment, and a funny thought came into my head: maybe she didn't blink too much because she didn't want to miss anything. Or maybe what she saw when she did close her eyes was something even she could get lost in, and she didn't want to do that unless she knew she was in a safe place herself.

I left her sitting alone on Casablanca's branch, dangling her rag-wrapped legs over the edge, and followed Rattail down and away. As I hit the soft wet grass, I thought I heard something odd: a steady patter that wasn't rain, becoming more solid, more rhythmic, like a horse. But there were no police on horses anywhere, as far as I could see in either direction.

"Hey. Going to Sharon Meadow?"

Casablanca popped out of one of the bushes by the tree. I swear, she's as tricky as the coyotes sometimes. I nodded at her, and she fell in beside me. "I'm coming, too," she told me.

We went east, not bothering to stay covered, just close enough to the bushes to duck in if we had to. I was edgy and nervous, and I didn't know why. After all, a sweep of the Cores didn't really affect me, unless they swept up Jesse. I couldn't see them doing that, because of who his father was. So why had Sal thought this was so important?

The answer was right there. If the Cores were pushed out of the park, the coyotes would go nuts. They'd lose their main source of easy food. They'd have to hunt for it, fight for it. Either that, or they'd spend more time outside the park, looking for garbage cans to get into, yards they could slip inside of, cats and small dogs they could steal.

Sal was right, and Angie had been right, too. This Mayor man wasn't too smart. If his idea was to get rid of the coyotes by starving them out of the park, he was pretty much condemning the rest of us in the park to be coyote food, and all the people who lived near the park were going to be really mad at him when coyotes started showing up in their yards, going through their trash, and stealing their pets to eat.

I followed Rattail to the edge of JFK Drive. We waited longer than I wanted to, exposed, right out there on the side of the road, until there was a break in the cars. Jesse had told me that the red signs stuck up at certain corners meant that cars have to stop there and wait until it's safe to go, but of course, that rule was about people for each other. It didn't apply to us, because they didn't have to stop for me. Besides, what with the rain and the light fading fast, we weren't about to take a chance on them not seeing us.

We took the long way around, next to the path Jesse had come down when the young coyote had treed me. We could tell right away that Sal had called it right: Sharon Meadow had about twenty police cars ringing it, and a lot of cops running around.

I don't know if they had all the Cores in the park out there—probably not, because there are a lot of people in the park who know how to stay hidden when they want to. But there were a lot of people, and most of them looked like the Cores. There's a look people get when they have to spend too much of their life outside. Humans aren't really good at doing that, so when they have to, it shows. Plus, there were the piles of stuff they had with them, sleeping rolls and shopping carts. And of course, a lot of them had dogs.

It was crazy, out there in the meadow. Most of the cops and the other official people were being nice about things, being patient, listening to what the

Cores were saying. I didn't see anyone trying to hurt anyone else, or any fighting. Some of the Cores were arguing, but no one was hitting anyone else.

We hung out and watched from a bush. The people nearest us was a group who had a couple of guys with them. I heard one of them tell one of the Cores that he was a doctor, they were all doctors, that they wanted to check out if the kids they were chasing out of the park were okay, or if they had anything wrong with them. That made me think of Jesse's father, who was in a hospital and who didn't like doctors touching him. I wondered if the Cores felt the same way about it.

I looked around, but I couldn't see Jesse anywhere. It was noisy and crowded and wet and cold, and I wondered what was going on in someone's head, why they'd stage something like this in the rain, when it was almost night. Maybe it was more silly stuff from the Mayor guy.

Ratty nudged me with his head. "Dark, look over there. It's the crazy-bad and his big scary dog. Looks like they're getting run out of the park."

He was right. It was Billy, shivering and soaked to the skin. He looked like he was having some kind of argument with the cop and the doctor. Both of them kept giving Nightmare nervous looks, but Nightmare was just sitting there. I thought he looked bored, then remembered what Jesse had said about Nightmare being actually okay, just stuck with a bad human for company.

The longer we stayed, the more the cops and the rest of the Blanks seemed to get organized with whatever it was they were doing. They looked at ID pictures and listened to people's chests with tubes. They took down names and asked questions. Some of the kids were put in the cop cars, and some of them had handcuffs put on them. I didn't know what that was about, but the feeling in the meadow was crazy-busy and sort of sad. . . .

"This is boring." Ratty was twitching. "Really boring. They're just going to kick all the Cores out, and what good does that do? They'll be back in about three days—they did this last year. I don't know why Sal thought we should come and watch this. Let's go back and wait for dinner, okay?"

'Blanca twitched. She was close enough to me so that I felt it. I turned and stared at her.

"What? 'Blanca? What's up?"

"Don't know. Something. Let's get out of here."

We headed out, walking west toward our tree. The wind was picking up. Even though we were on just the other side of the meadow, there were strange noises coming from all around us, loud enough to almost drown out some of the commotion on the other side of the tree line.

We'd reached the edge of the path now, standing right next to the tree I'd gone up the night Jesse had shooed away the young coyote. The wind was roaring now, and I heard a noise, a bad one, a sort of moaning and cracking. . . .

"Dark! Look out!"

I don't know why I jumped to the side instead of forward. Instinct, I guess, because really, I should have jumped straight ahead. And if I had, I would have been dead, because the branch that cracked free of the tree we'd stopped under landed just forward of where I'd been standing. It was a big, heavy branch, full of dead spiky twigs and hard knots in the wood.

"*Wow*-ow." Ratty was at my other side. "That was too close. Are you okay?"

"Maybe. I think so."

That was a lie. I wasn't okay. I wasn't hurt at all, but whatever had been pricking at Casablanca was pricking at me, too. Something was spooking me, and the problem was, I didn't know why. The tree thing was scary, but it wasn't enough to cause the prickling under my skin, the wanting to growl and hiss, the sense that something was all the way wrong, off, crazy-bad. The waterlogged branch that had just missed me had nothing to do with the sense that eyes were on me, following everything I did. It had come on suddenly, out of nowhere. I met 'Blanca's eye, and I saw she was feeling it, hard and tight.

I stepped sideways. My nerves were going nuts, humming out a warning, and I didn't know why. "Let's get out of here, all right? There's too many people out there, too much weirdness. I want to get back to our tree."

I ran across the street, moving fast. There were no cars, and I'd reached the other side and gone another half a block before I even realized that the other two were moving a lot more slowly than I was. Casablanca was behind Rattail, watching him walk.

"Dark, wait up. Ratty, are you okay?"

"I guess." He'd stopped. "My leg hurts, though."

"Oh, Ratty!" I'd been so tuned in to myself, listening to those weird signals, that I'd totally forgotten about his sore leg. He was hurting, and I hadn't noticed. "I'm a bad friend—I didn't mean to make it worse. Here, let me see—"

"Dark!"

Casablanca was moving. She wasn't coming toward me—she was in the middle of the road, heading back the way we'd just come, and she was going fast. She was calling my name, but I couldn't see her, because suddenly there was something else in my range of vision, and it took all my attention.

Something had come down from the hillside, not from the east where all the Cores and cops were, but from the west. It was large and pale. It ignored Rattail, frozen in place; it ignored Casablanca, flying across the street and up the tree I'd hidden in the first time it had hunted me. The big golden eyes were fixed on me, scenting me, knowing my scent.

"Dark!"

The thing between us stopped, turning for a moment, identifying where her voice was: the tree across the street. That gave me a second, just a moment of time.

"Run!"

There were plenty of trees within easy reach, but there was that humming in my nerves, the memory of the strong limb of our own tree giving way under Ratty's weight. I couldn't risk it. The tree I'd used to escape the coyote last time was the tree Casablanca was sitting in. It was sturdy and strong.

I jumped for the road. I was praying to Bastet, to whatever might be listening, anywhere and everywhere, hoping it could be heard over the noise of the wind and the people in the big meadow, just a minute away.

Oh, please please don't let it get me, don't let it catch me, please please please, move Dark, move like the wind moves in the trees, hard and fast . . .

Silence, nothing in my ears except for my own feet hitting the wet road surface, desperate not to slip. And then another sound, the only other sound in the world.

Breathing. It was no more than a body's length behind me. I could hear it. I could feel its heat, against my legs.

It was no good, and I knew it. The trees were close, so close—I could get there, but the coyote was right at my flank, and it was faster than I was, longer legs. It was very weird, but I could see it, even though I never stopped, never looked back, never wasted the extra second that would have taken: it was right at my side. I could feel the tendons in its neck snap into place as it stretched its muzzle and its jaws toward me, its breath moving the fur on my tail, preparing to grab me, take me down, tear me in half . . .

The breath became noise, a roaring, angry howl. It ripped through the rain, echoing through the trees.

All the noises I'd heard from the coyotes before had been high-pitched, almost squeaky. This sounded like the echoes you get when something falls into still water. It was low and deep and wailing, the sound of pain. It reminded me of Iris's howl, but it was different, too. Iris had howled with grief. This was rage, the sound of physical pain.

I was halfway up the tree, out of reach, turning my head. I was safe. 'Blanca, panting, was already on the branch. Up above me, I caught movement and saw something that shouldn't have been possible, something that made no sense: the flutter of tree-green rags, and a battered man's shoe.

But right then, I had no time to stop or think. Safe and alive, with my chest heaving and my heart trying to slam its way out of my body, I looked down and saw Ratty. He was airborne, being shaken like one of the branches in the wind, with his teeth clamped hard around the coyote's left rear leg.

"Ratty!" I don't think I'd ever made a noise like this one. I wondered if anyone in the meadow behind us could hear it, if Iris and her remaining pup could hear it, wherever in the trees behind us she'd made her lair. "Run, let go, let go, get out of there, get going, run run *run!*"

I don't know whether he heard me, or whether the timing was coincidence. But he let go and ran, not toward us but away from us to the east, back toward the thick bushes and trees on the other side, where the coyote had come from. He couldn't run toward us. The coyote was between him and our tree.

Cats have a thing we do, a trick, when we want to scare something off. We puff up, swelling our coats, making ourselves look twice our actual size. I'd never stopped to wonder whether other animals could do the same thing.

Down there, standing in the grass, the coyote suddenly doubled in size—or at least, it seemed to. Everything stood up and bristled. Even from up the tree, I could see that its rear leg, where Ratty had grabbed it, was a mess.

"Oh, no." 'Blanca was staring down. "Oh, no, no, no!"

The coyote turned and went for Rattail. Ratty was limping. The coyote, even with the mangled leg, didn't seem to be slowing down much.

A curtain of water, an empty road stretched out under the streetlights, a meadow full of police and Cores and doctors right behind us, Rattail running for his life, the coyote only a few feet behind and gaining fast, blood streaking down his leg and washing away down toward the storm drains . . .

I closed my eyes. There was nothing I could do, nothing at all except to not watch.

But I couldn't shut my ears. I couldn't keep the sound of what happened when the coyote made up

the lost ground and got Ratty between its jaws, adding Ratty's blood to the blood from its own wounded
leg. I still hear it sometimes, when I sleep.

For a moment, just one, there was something even
louder: thunder in my head, rhythmic, steady, the
sound of a thousand horses.

Then it was gone, and I opened my eyes, watching
the coyote slip up the hillside and away.

EPILOGUE

I can talk about all this now. I couldn't before—
it was too close, too much to think about.

Casablanca and I came down from the tree.
We were across the road, guarding Ratty, when a
familiar-sounding car turned the corner, on its way
to our usual feeding spot. I saw the car swerve, heard
the driver's-side window come down, heard Angie
from inside: *Oh my God, Jack, is that Dark and
Casablanca, what are they doing, oh God, oh no!*

So they found him, found us as we stood over our
friend, wailing. We were singing our friend to rest,
because yes, he was a raccoon and not a cat, but in
Bubastis there's a place for all those beloved of Bastet.
And every cat is Bastet.

So we sang him to his rest, while Jack got a towel out of the trunk of their car and wrapped Ratty in it, slow and careful, and Angie stood in the empty road, sobbing.

And Jack stayed with Ratty while Angie got back in the car and drove away. She came back with a shovel, the kind I'd seen the park gardeners using, and then she kept watch while Jack dug a grave under the tree Ratty had given me time to get to. I didn't know if Sal was still up there watching; I wasn't even sure she'd ever really been there.

They put Ratty into it, gently and carefully, and covered him over. *Deep enough so that the coyotes won't dig him up,* he told Angie, and she nodded, still crying, still fierce, agreeing with him. I looked at 'Blanca, and she looked back at me, and we were thinking the same thing. I never liked the Warms as much as I liked them then, with my heart breaking in half.

They fed us right there. No one and nothing had come by—not one car, not one person. We ate even more than we usually would. Ratty had died so that we could stay alive, and he would have been pretty upset with us if we'd starved ourselves as a way of saying "thank you." And they waited with us as the rain slowly tapered down to a light sprinkle and then to nothing and the wind died completely. Overhead, behind the canopy, I could see the clouds shredding, the first twinkle of stars.

"Going to my place." Casablanca seemed to have withdrawn into herself, even more than usual. "Want to?"

"No. Thanks, though. I just have this feeling I ought to stick around the park right now."

"Okay." She looked at me over her shoulder. "You heard horses?"

I stared at her. "Yes, I did, twice tonight. What's that about?"

"Choices," she told me. "Dark—take care of yourself."

Then she was gone, across the road and over toward JFK Drive. She was going to have a long way to go tonight, to get over and up the path to Fulton Street.

I was alone.

I didn't know what was driving me that night. It felt like the purest instinct I've ever known. There was no arguing with it: a voice that hit every hair, every nerve, every pore in my skin, told me things, and I followed.

Go and watch over Ratty, it told me, and I went. I wasn't worried about the coyotes or anything else. I just stood over the small soft mound of muddy earth Jack had shoveled over him and closed my eyes, remembering everything I could about him. Somewhere inside, I was also wondering about those horses I'd heard twice tonight. . . .

"Dark?"

I didn't turn my head. "Hey, Jesse. I was worried about you. Did you just get back to the park? Were you caught in the sweep tonight?"

"No. I was with my mother." He knew right away. I didn't have to tell him. "Oh, man. Rattail?"

"Yes."

The park would move on, seasons changing. The Cores coming back after a few days. Nothing else would change here, not really, The park's rhythms were about living, about dying.

"Is your mother okay? You were gone five days."

He'd knelt, settling his knees on the grass, resting one hand on Ratty's grave. "She's fine. My father's dead."

I looked up at him finally. I didn't say anything,

because I couldn't. Something strange was happening—I could hear the horses again, loud, so loud. And they seemed to be somewhere in the sky, but that was ridiculous, because horses don't fly. I wondered for a moment if it might be Memorie, the beat of her wings sounding like horses. But Casablanca had heard hoofbeats, too. It wasn't just me.

"He had cancer. Not what killed him, though, not really—he had a heart attack."

Hoofbeats—loud, soft, steady, up and down in my head. Jesse was watching me now. "I'm moving back in with my mom. Want to come?"

I stood still. Here came the horses, inches away, thundering across the heavens, they were in my tree, coming out of my tree . . .

A dangling shoe. Two shoes. Layers of green rags.

Sal came out of the tree. I watched her; Jesse watched her.

She shivered, one long tremor, and the green rags dropped away from her head, her arms, her bony black knuckles. She twisted, a strong ripple of muscle, straightening her back, stamping on the wet earth, kicking away the oversized cracked shoes. . . .

Black as coal, black as my own fur. She was no tiny thing, and no human being, either. She was huge and perfect.

A mane so long, it blew backward even while she stood still. A horse's head and face, with Sal's dark eyes watching me. Her neck arched toward the sky. Black hooves, as steady and strong on the ground as the roots of an oak tree.

It champed at the wet ground, marking the earth around the perimeter of Rattail's grave, four hooves sounding like thunder, loud, shaking the ground and shaking me.

It looked at me. The smile was Sal's smile.

There were wings overhead, the beat and rush of the owl, the rhythm of life and death in the park. Memorie's words came back to me, clear in my mind: *He is the Bringer and the Taker. When he is there for you, when you hear his music and he lets you see him, all your choices are made and over with.*

And then Memorie's voice was there, not only in my head, but in the air around me: *Your choices are made, cat. Go. I will see you safely out.*

I jumped for Jesse's jacket. He caught me, strong-handed and sure, and zipped me in, warm against the cold, dry against the wet. We walked south, southeast, past the meadow, past the carousel, past the Dumpsters, and out into the Haight, heading for home.

AFTERWORD

For ten years, my husband Nic and I have worked with the TNR cat-rescue group in Golden Gate Park, San Francisco's big city park. TNR stands for "Trap, Neuter, Release"—ensuring that these cats, most of whom are too feral to ever become pets, are healthy and safe, but not adding to the homeless cat population.

Of course, cats aren't the only animals in the park: we have raccoon families who recognize our car, run up and wait for us, knowing they're going to get fed. The park is home to possums, who keep the wasps' nests under control, and skunks, owls, and rabbits.

The foxes never hunted the cats; the cats didn't hunt the possums or the birds; the raccoons and skunks shared piles of food. All of them had an instinct that this kind of cooperation was the only way to stay alive.

One night in 2005, a cat we'd never seen before showed up at the park bench where we were already feeding a cream tabby named Ghost. The newcomer was pure black, with deep golden eyes, cautious but friendly, and she obviously knew people. I could tell, right away, that she was special. And I knew, right away, that her name was Dark.

Like most dedicated animal-rescue people, Nic and I are serious about it. We're in the park feeding our feral colony pretty much every night. Over the years, we've lost cats—to age, or illness, or people driving too fast. That's nature, the way life happens. It doesn't make us happy, but it's the normal cycle of things.

But in 2006, something happened that was outside that cycle.

First we heard from a few of the other TNR workers that some cats had been killed. From the looks of it, it seemed to be a dog. Everyone was very worried—a vicious dog is a danger. We drove around the park after feedings but saw no sign of anyone with a vicious dog. None of the homeless kids who lived in the park knew anything, either. They were as worried as we were.

The foxes began disappearing. That was scary, because the foxes were the top predator in the park. If something was killing them, it must be something really dangerous. We kept looking and asking, but no one knew anything.

Then a gardener was rushed to the hospital after she was swarmed and badly stung by yellowjackets. The possums had vanished—there was nothing controlling the nests.

Skunks disappeared. We would smell their spray, where they'd gotten into a fight, but they were in hiding. So were the waterbirds who usually walked along the lakeshores at night.

And then Ghost disappeared. Within a couple of days, the city's Animal Control office began getting frantic calls from people who jogged in Golden Gate Park or walked their dogs there or even just lived alongside: they'd seen what they thought were coyotes.

They were right. The park had been taken over by a couple of mating pairs of coyotes. These coyotes— who were new to the enclosed biosystem of the park—were wreaking havoc simply by doing what they do to stay alive: kill the competition, and eat anything they can catch.

Our calls to Animal Control and the mayor's office were ignored. Coyotes jumped out from behind trees and bushes, charging at people with dogs on leashes. More park animals were killed. No one with the authority to act wanted to do anything at all.

Then one night, we drove up to feed Dark and her new buddy, a old, smart feral named Ivy. We were just in time to see a young coyote charging straight at them.

That was the point at which I knew Dark's story needed to be told—for her sake, for the rest of the animals, and for the coyotes, too. As I write this, there are still coyotes in the park. The TNR group has managed to catch and relocate many of the park cats to a wonderful shelter in the California hills. More skunks are around, but they're cautious and we haven't seen a possum or a fox for over a year now.

The park is a different place than it was the first night we met Dark. This is her story.

DEBORAH GRABIEN has lived, worked, and hung out all over Europe—from London to Geneva to Paris to Florence. But San Francisco has always been home, and she returned to the city for good in 1981. These days, in between cat rescues and cookery, Deborah can generally be found listening to music, playing music on one of eleven guitars, hanging out with her musician friends, or writing fiction. You can visit her online at www.deborahgrabien.com.